Pax Titanus

THE NEW BIZARRO AUTHOR SERIES
PRESENTS

Pax Titanus

Tom Lucas

Eraserhead Press
Portland, OR

Eraserhead Press
P.O. Box 10065
Portland, OR 97296

WWW.ERASERHEADPRESS.COM

ISBN: 1-62105-164-1

Editor's Note

Tom Lucas.

Remember this name; you're going to be seeing a lot of great fiction from this guy.

I first read *Pax Titanus* as a short story, and it was a great short story: laugh out loud funny, fun and creative, and it pulled at my heart strings. Of course it had to become a longer work.

Luckily, for you and for me, Tom was willing to accommodate my request and write *Pax Titanus* as a full-on novella for the New Bizarro Author Series.

I love this book. I love the exploration of the different alien races and the cultures; this element of Tom's writing is reminiscent of Douglas Adams. I love the humor, I love the characters, I love the story and the plot arc. It's a great ride, and I'm so excited you get to join in on it.

I'm happy to present Tom Lucas' book to you as part of the New Bizarro Author Series. This is this author's first book with Eraserhead Press! The NBAS strives to bring new voices in bizarro fiction to our readers; it serves as an opportunity to introduce you to new writers. Eraserhead Press is happy to bring new, weird voices to you in the hopes that these authors will prove themselves to be strong members of the bizarro community and continue to entertain you for years to come. The publishing of this book marks the beginning of a one year proving period. Please help support our NBAS writers in their endeavors by telling your friends about their cool new books, posting reviews online and sharing the books via social media. This book you hold is only one of several hundred that must be sold in order for this author to continue on his path. I hope you help him along as best as you can. Thank you.

~Spike Marlowe

For Toby.

Special thanks to Team Teatro Bizarro.

CHAPTER ONE

Craxx and Titanus were best friends. It was just a matter of time before Craxx wrapped his stubby fingers around Titanus's massive red cock.

The two had been partners for years. They worked construction jobs from one end of the galaxy to the other, and they were good at what they did. They had helped build the Party Pyramids of Quantos IV, the Plasma Canals of Gynerous, as well as less impressive structures such as the Trailer Parks of Mentoz.

There was an unspoken understanding between them, that rare thing that so few find in their partners. If Titanus needed a tool, Craxx was already handing it to him before he asked. If Craxx needed an extra hand, Titanus knew to offer him one, two, or all four of his. Titanus trusted Craxx implicitly, and Craxx never let him down.

Craxx had been there for the birth of Titanus's son, Tinyanus. Titanus had helped Craxx when his big mouth had gotten him into trouble with, well, everyone he had ever met.

They had what most call chemistry. Most likely it came from their differences. Titanus was Veritassian, a race known for their inability to state anything but the truth. Craxx was Delbian, curious creatures who are compelled to say exactly what they are thinking, even when it isn't relevant to the conversation at hand.

"I took an amazing shit today, Tits," Craxx said as the two walked up to their latest assignment, a quick repair on an Atomic Elevator.

"I don't care," said Titanus.

Craxx laughed. "I know, but surely you can appreciate the need for regularity."

Titanus grunted.

"I've been thinking a lot about my sister."

"Stop. You've talked about this before. It's unnatural."

Craxx stammered, then blurted, "I don't think I've seen a better ass. I want to rub it down with scented oils."

Titanus didn't acknowledge the thought. It wouldn't help if he did. The more embarrassing or uncomfortable statements usually fell off once they started the work. This was just pre-gig babble. The thought did make Titanus shudder, but he refused to reveal that fact.

Times had been a bit rough of late for the two. An intergalactic recession had meant less work, and they had been forced to take any job they could find, no matter what the risk. Space elevators, atomic ones, were particularly dangerous.

They stood at its base and looked up. The job was far above their heads.

Craxx rubbed his big, blue belly. He was only wearing pants today, giving his flabby rolls of fat permission to roam free. "Who puts an atomic reactor a mile above the surface anyway? If the thing blows, doesn't it just poison the atmosphere? It's a piñata of death. These people are idiots. I have to fart."

Titanus tightened his tool belt, using a free hand to hold his nose. Craxx's gas could be sold to the Emperor's army for crowd control. Most foul. "Their stupidity led to us getting some work today," he countered. "It's a simple job, really. We just have to reinforce the mounts. Apparently it has developed a bit of a wobble."

"Ok. Hey man, you been working out? You are looking seriously ripped."

"No." Titanus extended one his four arms to Craxx. "Now hold on, I'm going to engage the lifters." Craxx held his hand out, but his stubby arm couldn't reach. Titanus made his arm just a bit longer, grabbed him by the wrist, and pushed them upwards.

"I never get tired of that trick, Tits. Man, does my ass stink! It's swampy and foul. I need to stop eating cheese."

Up they went.

◆◆◆

"This doesn't look right," said Titanus. The mounts that held the reactor in place were missing half of the required bolts.

"Maybe Space Carnies put this shit together." Craxx's eyes darted about. "Heh."

Titanus ran his finger along the holes, and then studied the tips. "Clean. There were bolts here. They have been removed."

"Shit. Why do I want to fuck my sister?"

"Craxx, you are a friend. I need you to do your best not to speak for a moment. Please."

Craxx nodded and zipped his thick lips tight. The muscles in his face strained as they fought to keep his jaw shut. He puffed his cheeks. He was clearly fighting a follow up thought. Titanus slowly navigated the beams. Below him, the swirls of purple and orange clouds hid the surface of the planet from view, a serene ocean of color that contrasted the danger of the situation at hand.

"I do not understand why this tower has not collapsed," Titanus said under his breath. "It was poorly constructed and it is missing vital braces."

In response, the beam beneath his feet dropped slightly.

"Careful!" Craxx screamed. "My sister has a friend who—"

His hand flew up to his mouth. He mumbled something that sounded like an apology.

Titanus moved back slightly. The first creak was barely audible, and then came the nauseating, high-pitched screech of metal on metal as two beams began to grind into one another. Then another creak, from a far beam. Then three more in quick succession from a crisscross beam directly below. The reactor, a simple steel box, shifted on its platform, humming quietly, oblivious to everything happening around it.

Titanus frowned. "This elevator tower is about to fall apart, Craxx. We need to disconnect the reactor. Are you familiar with the procedure?"

Craxx nodded yes. "Before we teamed up I used to maintain Nexus power couplets. Similar set up. What do you need me to do?"

A pressure tube snapped, releasing small droplets of coolant. They gently floated away, small green pearls into the ether.

"Ok, I'm going to come around the other side and—"

The beam below Craxx's feet gave way, snapping off and away. Snagged by a giant invisible hand, it disappeared into the clouds. Craxx fell to a small platform directly below. The blue reptilian smiled, a thousand small daggers gleaming in the starlight. "Ha! Thought I was a goner, didn't 'cha?"

Titanus looked to him, then the reactor. "Don't move, friend. I am going to secure that thing." Using all four of his arms, as well as his legs, he began to spider climb along the girders and metalwork, using careful and deliberate movements. "Almost there. We will be successful."

As Titanus gripped the reactor box, his sense of achievement evaporated as he felt the upper portion of the elevator's skeletal frame give way, punctuated by the rapid, machine gun sound of a thousand welds snapping. He held the reactor securely, unsure of what to do next.

With nothing to hold them, the approaching ground beckoned.

Craxx let out a pathetic squeal. "I can't die now! I got shit to do!" The two friends fell parallel to one another; Craxx's face the portrait of fear. "Tits, I gotta tell you something."

"Let's concentrate on living," Titanus said, straining to pull the reactor to his chest, the force of free fall making its presence known. "We've got a mile to figure it out."

Craxx was babbling, crying. He couldn't focus when he was calm, and now he was hysterical. "Oh god, oh god. We are going to die! Get big, Tits, get big!"

Titanus cleared his mind, pushing out the alarming sensation of the building speed of his descent. They were passing through the clouds and the lack of visual input helped. If only he could filter out his friend's high-pitched screams, but that would not be an option.

Enlarge! He focused his thoughts first on his upper arms. Deep within his flesh, his Veritassian DNA began to heat and accelerate cellular growth. Like a spark into a fire, his bone and flesh began to grow, forcing his tough skin to stretch in accommodation. A growing orange glow swirled about him. A lightning storm of energy began to crackle and with that, the size of his upper arms tripled in an instant. The reactor was safe.

They had broken through the clouds. Craxx was directly speaking to whatever god he had, begging forgiveness for a lifetime of nearly uninterrupted carnal thoughts. Titanus cleared his mind a second time, sweeping away the distraction of exertion and forced his other two arms to stretch far beyond their normal means. The orange lighting cracked again. To either side, his arms pushed out until they found one of the elevator's support poles. It wouldn't stop his fall, but it would slow it considerably.

That left Craxx, who was now falling much faster than Titanus. His short, stubby arms flailed with futility. Titanus, who had the reactor clutched safely, and something to slow the fall, could now concentrate fully on saving his oldest and dearest friend.

In a move that clearly showed his love for the Delbian, Titanus emptied his mind a third time and focused on the growth of the only free appendage he had remaining, his cock. As he had practiced the technique multiple times as a teenager, the sudden increase in the girth and length of his member was nearly second nature, although he would have to push it further than ever before. He closed his eyes as he felt his member swell and harden. His mighty helmet tore through his work pants with little regard, a true solider that would not be held back by such a flimsy obstruction.

Now free, his monstrous and veiny bangstick flew forward, with Craxx dead in its sites. "As soon as you can, grab on!"

Craxx moaned. "Really, this is how you do this? Save me with your custard chucker? Ah fuck."

The planet's surface was in full view. "No time. Say hello to Captain Winky or kiss dirt, my friend."

His friend obliged. As soon as Titanus's telephone pole was within reach, Craxx latched on.

"It's so smooth. Your wife's pussy must secrete skin moisturizer." Titanus chuckled. "Actually, it does."

"It's hard to find a grip, I keep sliding around. You're getting really hard." He raised his eyebrows. "I think you kinda like this."

"Do your best to hold on. I've got the reactor and I've slowed our fall, but now I have to brace us for it. I will begin reeling you in as I transfer that growth energy to my back, to make a temporary turtle shell to shield us from impact. And yes, it does feel good. Stop moving so much."

"You spooge on me and I'll kick your ass. Hey Tits, I got a question."

"NO TIME FOR QUESTIONS. STOP MOVING!"

"Does your wife have any friends? My penis isn't nearly this smooth and kissable."

◆◆◆

The fine citizens of Glorbo 18 loved their pop music. At first, its proliferation only resulted in a small downtick in the overall IQ of the population, but over time it had become a blend of obsession and religion, if one could even make the distinction.

Today was the highest of all holidays, the final day of a festival known as the Daze of Atonement. A mind-numbing week of musical celebration and self-flagellation, its purpose was to acknowledge the fact that what the Glorboians loved was so very terrible and that they should be punished for it. The festival included public admissions of guilt, light torture and whipping, and of course, intricately choreographed dance numbers. Set over a series of a hundred stages, it would have been impressive if it weren't for the fact that the music was so awful.

Noted Glorboian Diva, Hickey Lamange, was about to begin the final of twenty encores, a complex piece that involved fifteen costume changes, live animals, and an egg tossing contest between her dancers and robotic pigs. A single spotlight highlighted her form. Silent, she stood with her back to the crowd to amp up the dramatic effect. A beat dropped and a lonely voice sang a single note. The crowed erupted in joy for they knew that she was about to perform her greatest hit, "LUV ain't just the AZZ. Itz th' PANK 2."

It was a tender ballad. Critics had praised it, noting that it was rich with metaphor and imagery.

Fortunately for Titanus and Craxx, she stood in the perfect place to cushion their fall from high above. Red hot from reentry, Titanus's enlarged back muscles squashed Hickey so completely that all that remained was a gelatinous puddle of viscera and glitter. The crowd, not completely understanding that their beloved diva was now leaking through the cracks of the damaged stage, thought the unexpected crash of the construction workers was a part of the act.

And when Titanus's fuck stick exploded, hosing Veritassian Man Gravy all over Craxx and the first five rows of the audience, the tattooed and unwashed masses went berserk. Holorecording Communicators flew out from pockets, pouches, and bags. The moment was captured forever, viewed instantly by what was later estimated to be quadrillion galactic citizens.

The rioting crowd proceeded to tear apart the barricades in an attempt to get closer to the two friends. Craxx wiped the jizz from his eyes. "Seriously, what the fuck man? Your spunk smells like creamsicle. "He smacked his fat lips. "But it don't taste like 'em."

Titanus paused, calling back his enlarged anatomy until he was back to his normal, 10-foot tall, four armed, and bruising self. He clutched the atomic reactor. It had never moved. He had saved it, his friend, and the citizens of Glorbo 18. It had only cost one diva, one that would eventually become a mourned legend. She would also manage to release twelve more albums posthumously and absolutely no one would ever question how that was possible.

"I told you to stop moving. I couldn't help it. You have magic fingers," said Titanus. "Look at this crowd, Craxx, they are so happy to be alive."

The audience was rioting, but it was an upbeat riot meant to show their appreciation. That day, there were twenty trampling deaths, a fire that burned for months after, and three thousand documented cases of Arenuian Herpes.

14

"They think this is a part of the show, Tits. You're going to be famous. You'll be known around the galaxy for what you have done. I'm fucking jealous. You're going to get a lot of pussy. Groupies! Groupies! Groupies!"

"I'm not interested in that," said Titanus. "I don't want the attention. No one should be celebrated for doing the right thing."

Craxx finally had the last of the sperm wiped off. "You're not going to get a choice buddy. This kinda shit always goes viral. Now, you're buddy Craxx knows how these things work, so let me help you. We need to get you the hell out of here. The base of the elevator can't be too far off. Let's make a run for it. We might be able to make it home before the media figures out who you are and where you live. And maybe your wife can secrete some moisturizer for me? If I ask nice? I want a smooth dick like yours."

CHAPTER TWO

Titanus piloted his hovertruck in a languid circle on the outskirts of the asteroid belt.

"Well, nothing on sensors. Looks quiet."

Craxx was fiddling with his holorecorder. "Well, your name is all over the place. Let's hope it stays that way. When I was a kid, I crapped my pants. Every day. The wet ones were the worst. All the kids in the school called me Butt Craxx."

"I'm pulling in."

The sight of his humble home, a series of domes and tunnels, made with his own four hands, was a welcome vista. Inside, his wife and child. Dinner. And his bed. Titanus parked the truck and handed the keys to Craxx.

"Take it, I'm not going anywhere tonight. Pick me up tomorrow."

"Aw, buddy. I wanted to come in and say hello to the lovely wife. She's the hottest squid I know. I'd do her. Upside-down and backwards."

"Friend, really? You have no control whatsoever?"

Craxx rubbed his jaw. "Nope, from brain to mouth. I am what I am. I'll see you in the morning."

Titanus grabbed his toolbox from the bed of the truck, gave Craxx a quick salute and went inside. The comfort of familiar routine would certainly help to remove the stress of the day. He hung his tool belt on the third hook just inside the airlock door and dropped a wrench in the bowl he used to keep all his odds and ends.

Plopping down on a reinforced steel bench, he pried off one boot, then the other. Then he peeled off both socks and flung them into a basket. He took a deep breath and released it slowly.

The day had been more risky than most. If life were truly fair, he wouldn't have made it home. Titanus took a minute to consider the photo he hung to the right of the door. In it, the whole family, taken on the kid's first birthday. Between his muscular girth and his wife's long, squid-like body, the background was completely blotted out, not that it mattered. What was important was that he could see his wife's true beauty; she had such wonderfully huge round eyes that contrasted her elongated skull and sharp beak. Cradled by both parents, their small child laughed.

It was time for the real thing. Titanus yanked the inner door open and announced his arrival. He was immediately tackled by a sea of flailing and flopping tentacles and covered with suction cup kisses.

"Hiediiee," Titanus said relieved. This was not her true name, but Titanus lacked the proper anatomy to pronounce it. "What I day I have had."

Her multiple appendages tightened. Within moments, he could feel her secretions. There were so many. She was excited, nervous, proud, and feeling slightly constipated.

"I know," he said, running his hands over her body mass. "I gamble with my safety sometimes. But when I take a job, I do the job. This one just got out of hand."

Her grip grew tighter. Titanus felt her attach to any available flesh. Five minutes later, and the tears began to flow. His stomach cramped. "Yes," he said. "Craxx did get some jewelry today. A pure Veritassian Pearl Necklace!" He exploded with laughter. She had such a wonderful sense of humor.

"Now where's my boy?"

"Daddy!" came a voice from around the corner.

"Is that the mighty Tinyanus I hear?

A giggle erupted down by his feet. He looked but saw nothing. "I thought I heard something, but I don't see..."

Hearing a giggle from behind him. Titanus turned around with a jolt, but nothing was there either. He rubbed his big, bald head. "Where could that boy be? It's time for dinner."

From above, a small creature dropped onto his back. Titanus felt his son's little arms struggle to hold on at first, but he quickly held fast. Without a word, Titanus began to trot around the kitchen.

"That's a fine steed," Tinyanus said. He pretended to whip his father's back. "Heeyah!"

"I love you, son. I'm so glad to be home tonight."

◆◆◆

These were the times that Titanus cherished most. Sitting at the table with his family. Good food. Tinyanus playing with small toy warriors. Hiediiee quietly absorbing her food. Normally, he would never turn on the holomonitor, but after the day's excitement he could not deny his curiosity.

The news was typical. Footage of Fringe Rebels blowing up Newmonian Salt Refineries. Lots of tits and ass. A short segment on the cutest furry beasts of Quadrant 29.

And live cameras in front of Titanus's house.

Fuck.

Titanus coughed, choking on his food. "We're on holovid."

"Really?" Tinyanus squealed and ran to a window, waving frantically. "Daddy, can you see me waving on the monitor? Can they see me?"

"Get away from the windows!" Titanus yelled as he hit the button that turned on the plasma shields. "The media are here. They are vultures."

"Whooo, we're famous Daddy!" Tinyanus jumped up and down. "This is awesome!"

Titanus motioned for his son to calm down. Hiediiee slithered over to the window control and lowered the meteorite blinds. They were now completely locked down. Titanus studied the monitor.

"Looks like about thirty of them. Live broadcasters. About a thousand more drones."

The gaggle of reporters waited at the end of driveway. At least they were polite. However, there would be no leaving the home without going through them. On screen, Bradley Perfection, the top intergalactic anchorman, reported the rescue of the Glorboian reactor as well as the tragic death of singer Hickey Lamange.

The anchorman laughed with vigor.

"It's a bit of a push pull, people. Lose a diva, keep a planet."

Bradley ran his hand through his plastic hair.

"Currently we have reporters waiting outside the home of Titanus, the Veritassian responsible for saving the planet. As soon as we are able to defeat his home's defense grid, we should get a few words from this unlikely hero. But first, here's a message from Auntie Nuke's. 'If your food ain't glowin' then it ain't Auntie Nuke's.' We'll be right back."

Titanus almost always knew what to say. When he didn't, he said nothing. He studied the monitor in silence. On the horizon, the silhouettes of several heavy military craft could be seen. They were on a fast attack approach. Titanus pointed at the screen.

"Come to me, family. We are about to get hit. The shields should hold."

Huddled, the three braced for impact. The thunder of rockets hammering the ground and the deep rumble of earth shattering explosions shook them to the bones but their home remained intact. Titanus glanced up on the screen. The reporters were no longer there. Instead, there was a large, smoking crater. Only a single, singed cameraman remained but he quickly ran away. Bradley Perfection was screaming something about the ultimate sacrifice and then the footage cut to a commercial for an industrial-size butt massager.

There was a knock at the door.

"Imperial Guard. Open up!

Titanus obliged. He made a wall with three of his arms to protect his wife and child.

A small unit of Guardsmen stood on the front porch. In their one-ton powered armor suits, they were quite formidable, even when you are ten feet tall.

"Titanus of Veritassia?"

Titanus nodded.

"On behalf of the Emperor of the Universe, I hereby invite you to his court. You have caught his eye with your recent heroics. You are free to bring your family, if you wish." The Guardsman popped his visor open with an efficient snap of the wrist. "Also, my men will clean up this mess. You will have to forgive us. It's just too much fun blowing up journalists. I'm sure you can understand."

Titanus did not, but accepted the invitation nonetheless.

CHAPTER THREE

Ten armored guards walked on either side of Titanus. They did not speak. There was only the click-clack of their heavy boots on the ornate tile floor. He had seen footage of the Imperial Palace on the holomonitor many times. The Emperor was quite fond of making appearances as well as showing off his fancy digs. Although it was far too colorful for Titanus's taste, he did admire the quality of construction. It was truly an architectural masterpiece. There were subtle flashes of design that he had only read about in books, curious angles meeting in impossible corners. Delicate lighting. Complex mosaics that illustrated 50,000 years of intergalactic and multi-dimensional history. Titanus was suitably awed by the craftsmanship.

The guards guided him to a large iron door. Their captain removed his gauntlet, twiddled his fingers, and with a loose wrist, tapped on the door with his knuckles.

"Knock, knock. Knockity knock knock knock. Knock," he said.

"Did you just say the word knock for each tap on the door?" Titanus asked.

The captain shrugged sheepishly and took two steps back. He held his hand out to Titanus. "Wait."

Titanus stood in front of the massive door and kept his eyes focused upon its knob. In the periphery of his vision, he noticed the guards quietly taking steps backward. They were putting as much distance between them and the door as possible.

"I see what you are doing," Titanus muttered under his breath.

They continued to shuffle backwards in silence.

The door swung open with a dramatic creep and creak. He stepped inside. Looking around, the room felt more like the deep bowels of a temple or some kind of shrine. It did not look like a court or reception chamber. On the far wall, as far away from the door as one could be, a wizened and gray-bearded humanoid, roughly three feet in height, stood at a pedestal. He was scribbling madly into a book.

"Have a seat, my son."

Titanus spied an overstuffed purple velour lounger and did his best to make his anatomy work as it was on the smallish size. He felt ridiculous with his knees at chest level, but short of sitting on the floor, it was the best he was going to do. The furniture was for a diminutive man such as the Emperor, and not a big lug like him.

"Comfortable?"

"No. But I will make do."

"I suppose that will have to be good enough."

"You've asked for my presence. Now you have it. What is it that you wish to speak to me about?"

"My, my, you are blunt. Please relax. This was intended as a friendly meeting. We are just two men speaking. Normal men, with normal interests, and normal hobbies. Like mine, which I was enjoying when you arrived."

"I suppose you would like me to ask about your hobby? Does it relate to that book of yours?"

"Why yes, my book. Very perceptive. I was recording some new information in it when you came in. I was writing in my Vajournal."

"Vajournal. I do not know what kind of thing that is."

"Let me explain. I am recording the moisture state of every vagina in the universe, one snatch at a time. I am also noting variations in internal temperatures and viscosity. It relaxes my mind. There is a lot of twat in the universe —my universe."

Titanus quickly played out every possible response, but they all ended with death, either his or the Emperor's. He elected to say nothing.

"Yes, it is remarkable. And you know what else is remarkable? You." The Emperor smiled, but there was no happiness behind it. "Wine?"

Titanus shook his head.

"Ah, suit yourself. I'll have one of my servants bring you some fruit juice, seeing as how you are big pussy. I should put you in my Vajournal."

Titanus began to stand.

"Oh sit, I jest. I was just curious as to what you would do," said the Emperor with a wink. Behind him, cabinets formed out of nothingness. They were made of a rich, dark wood. Gorgeous. From them, he pulled out a large, green-glassed bottle. "Bartonian Red? That looks about right." In his empty right hand, a glass appeared and Titanus watched with as the wine poured itself.

"Neat trick, right? You don't get to be the Emperor of the Universe without a few. Tell me, what do you see?"

"An old man."

"And tell me, what did you expect to see, on your travel to my palace?"

"An old man. I have see holos of you before. Many times."

"And is that what you truly see?"

"I don't understand your question."

"Look carefully," the Emperor said as his face began to melt away.

"Your face is dissolving."

The remainder of the Emperor's form fell away. In its place, a hairy screaming beast. Then, a disembodied head, blood dripping from its neck, mouth open but not making a sound. This faded away into the form of a crying human child before becoming a hovering ball of white-hot plasma. The plasma returned to the figure of the old man.

"That is my true form, son. Plasma. Now watch the walls." They too dissipated, and in their place, barren stone coated with a filthy mold and soot.

Then it all returned.

"You see what I want you to see. You see what I know you want to see. There is more to this world than you could ever know."

"I know only truth and that has always been good enough. Your abilities are curious, but disappointing. None of this is real."

The Emperor laughed. "It's all real, in its own way. Oh, that's what I love about you Veritassians. You state your feelings clearly. You are an honest and succinct race. Most people who meet me just babble on and on."

"Thank you. We are."

The Emperor laughed more. "Spot on. Now, I ask you, do you enjoy your life?"

"Yes. I have a beautiful wife and child who fill my heart with joy. I am talented in my work and it brings me great satisfaction."

"Good, good. And there has been peace in your quadrant? A quiet neighborhood?"

"My asteroid home is remote, so yes."

"Not all have that luxury. There are those that threaten the peace. A peace that spans all that I rule. All of the known universe."

"You speak of the rebels? They are fools."

"They are dangerous fools. They are getting into the heads of the people. Corrupting their thoughts. Stealing their thoughts. Giving them new ones. Dangerous ones. They attack on the fringes, but their propaganda reaches into the inner rims of my empire. I am determined to kill every last one of them. I'll hang them by their own entrails and feed their sex organs to the dogs. Or their families. I haven't decided about that last part."

Titanus pointed at the wine bottle. "I'll have some of that now."

The Emperor poured him a glass.

"I've been dealing with them for some time but they have proven to be very resourceful. That's why I have called you here. I need your help, Titanus."

Titanus swallowed the wine in a single gulp and then motioned for more. "I don't know how I could help you. I am not a warrior. I am a peaceful man. I only fight when I forced to."

"You will not need to fight, but you will have to stand tall, my son. I will be naming you the 'Citizen's Champion' tomorrow. Your heroics in saving those silly Glorboites, er, Glorboians, err, fuck, whatever you call them, has made you a media sensation. You probably have no idea, but that ridiculously large cock of yours has made quite a splash, so to speak. I need that cock, as well as the man attached to it. I'm putting you on a goodwill tour of sorts. Promote teamwork amongst the citizens. Show how well the empire treats them. Make them secure in the status quo." The emperor was now pacing the room. "Really give them the warm and fuzzies. Right in the old cockles." He paused in mid-thought. "A cock for cockles. Ha!"

The Emperor shuffled back to the far edge of the room and returned to scribbling into his book.

"I don't think I'm your man, sir. I cannot portray the falsehoods you wish to employ."

"You don't have to be my man, you have to be theirs. It won't be a difficult job. You'll see." His nose pressed to the page. He made a mark, and then erased it. "What was her name? The one with the really drippy slit? Kinda yeasty?" He scratched at the side of his head.

"And if I should fail?"

"Hmm? Oh, you die. Your family dies. You know I don't tolerate failure."

Titanus winced. "And if I refuse?"

"Same." The old man was now writing at a furious pace.

"So no choice. Fine. So be it."

"Fear not, you're going to be stellar! I got a feeling about you. Besides, you and your family will be financially rewarded for your efforts. Now get the fuck out. I'm really struggling to describe Falffalian labia. Their clams are super funky."

Titanus left the Emperor to his work. The room may or not have faded out of existence after he closed the door behind him.

CHAPTER FOUR

All of the Emperor's public appearances were tedious and self-indulgent. The award ceremony was no different. The show began with his six-hour speech/monologue/amateur standup comedy performance. Only the Emperor laughed at the jokes, and as he was the one delivering them, it was rather awkward. When his royalness shifted gears and performed his one-man interpretive dance recital, the general vibe of the crowd was hardcore-mode uncomfortable. The only thing that broke the tension was the hour of public executions.

A few were darkly entertaining.

Eventually Titanus was brought to the stage, given a medal for his bravery, and named "Citizen's Champion." As there had never been one before, most of the universe was quite puzzled by what it all meant, but they put their doubts aside and mainly concentrated on trying to get Titanus to drop his pants. In many ways, his cock was the true celebrity. Had Titanus the opportunity to detach his member and leave, hardly anyone would have noticed his departure.

No good deed goes unpunished, and this was no exception. The difficulty in choosing to leave his family at home, under Craxx's watchful eye, was immense. Hiediiee had needed metric tons of consoling. The idea of a galactic tour had been too much for the girl. Titanus had held her for days while she secreted gallons of concern. They had never been apart for long. He was not pleased to leave either and through the magic of her chemical communications, they understood their love in a manner so profoundly more complex that spoken conversation could ever express. It was moments of realization such as these that left Titanus with the understanding that words are rather cheap in the face of oily enzymatic seepage.

After a bit more tentacle wringing, Titanus left his asteroid home. He would do the tour alone, but with a strong sense of purpose, for he at least he would providing for his family. He hopped into the shuttlecraft the Emperor had sent for him and took a long look out of the window as it began its quiet ascent into the inky abyss of space. There his wonderful wife and son stood, her waving her multiple appendages wildly; his son was bouncing up and down. With so many limbs flying about, it looked like a small party had gathered for his departure. In contrast, Craxx just stood there, nervous smile across his face.

Titanus felt a single tear roll down his cheek. There must have been something in his eye.

◆◆◆

Skoptic 7, The Outer Rim: a blue-collar planet in a economically depressed system. As it was far from the Capital Planet, with few resources and little Imperial support, the thought was that they could use a big motivational kick in the pants. Without any prep, Titanus was shoved out on the stage, in front of a million live Skoptics and 6 billion in the viewing audience, plus one. The Emperor would be watching.

Hesitantly, Titanus walked to a lonely microphone set in the middle of the stage. Behind him, an enormous holomonitor replayed his gallant use of his man baster on Glorbo 18. A small but tight live band that used small animals as instruments tried to energize the audience. The cacophony of screeches, squeals, and barks worked well to hide Titanus's nervousness.

"Um, Hello Skoptic 7," said Titanus.

The crowd was silent. A slight loop of feedback fired brain darts out of the sound system. Titanus tapped the microphone. He could hear a steady beat through his monitor. The microphone was working.

"Happy to be here." He wiped the sweat off his thick brow. Tough crowd.

A voice, from somewhere slightly middle and perhaps a bit to the left, called out. "Are you? Why are you here, anyway?"

Titanus looked to stage right. His handlers stared at their shoes and clipboards. One of them whistled conspicuously and inched back behind some crates. They weren't any help at all and neither were his Veritassian manners.

"Well, my understanding is that your lives are super shitty and I'm here, as a commoner myself, to show you that life is pretty good."

Sneers and catcalls followed. "Our lives are shitty, huh? You know all about us?"

"Well no, but look at you. You are dirty people. Filthy." He motioned to the buildings that surrounded the city square. "Your buildings are poorly constructed and show no signs of maintenance. As a construction worker, I have little respect for your abilities. Really, you people suck at life."

What some would later call a minor kerfuffle ensued, although others preferred to describe it as "glorious chaos" and "sexy mayhem." Titanus was quickly rushed offstage and strippers of all three Skoptic genders were put in his place. It took several live sex acts to get the crowd back into order. Bushels of local currency were dropped on the angry crowd by gyrocopter, along with a weaponized aerosol sedative.

A debacle on the first stop, with so many more to go.

Upset, the Emperor assigned his greatest spin doctors to around the clock to deal with Titanus's brutal honesty. They could not keep up, and one by one they were executed and replaced. Handlers came and went as well. Still, the big red man of Veritass was kept on the road. It was hoped that the constant hammering of appearances, interviews, dream insertions, psychic projections, and virtual reality recreations would exhaust his tendency to plant his foot deeply into his mouth. Titanus had a way with words, he truly did, and it just was that his way with words had the pleasing effect of a dry fist fuck.

The tour, and the concept of a "Citizens' Champion" was, as favorite pudgy pundit Gappt Storkel put, "A flaming, screaming piece of radioactive pterodactyl shit thrown into the face of a diseased and dying orphan." The Emperor would call it "A Fucking Disaster of Monumental Fucktitude with Fuck Sauce and Sprinkles of Fuck on Top."

Titanus desperately wanted to go home. An unexpected communication from his wife gave him an important reason to do so.

CHAPTER FIVE

Titanus didn't wait for the sanitizer unit to complete its cycle. He was far too worried. He pushed his way through the series of three doors that comprised the rear airlock of his home. Hiediiee waited in the foyer for him. The pool of her fluids underneath her pseudopods confirmed his worries.

The moment that she saw him, she flung her mass forward, landing securely onto his torso. She wrapped herself around him and squeezed tightly. If it weren't for his massive quad-pectorals, she would have choked him. His thickness gave her permission to crush him with abandon.

Titanus found her nerve cluster and gently gripped it with his upper hands. He gave it the slow brain massage, something that had always given her great comfort in the past. With every one of her suction cups attached to his generous muscles, she let herself get completely wet.

The range of emotions that he absorbed from her would have been, in another context, awe-inspiring. Here and now, it made him weep.

"How long has he been like this?"

She squeezed him twenty times, which meant twenty hours. He carried her with him to Tinyanus's room. Lying in his bed, surrounded by his toys, he seemed to be sleeping peacefully, but he was not alone in his room. In the corners, if one did not look directly at them but kept their gaze to the peripheral, the movement of translucent and nondescript blue forms could be seen.

Dream Leeches.

"Fuck," whispered Titanus. Hiediiee held tight, pure woe being pumped from her veins into his.

Dream Leeches couldn't be killed by any means known to the Veritassian. They did not exist in normal time-space. They lived off dreams, both good and bad. They could only be removed by those who had summoned them and were used specifically to trap a person's consciousness, for one dreadful purpose or another.

"Craxx?" asked Titanus. "Where's Craxx?"

She did not know.

"Relax. It's going to be ok, my love. Don't get all knotted up."

He said this because he believed it. He forced himself to believe it. Whoever was responsible would arrive soon. He would be ready for them.

◆◆◆

Desperate, they lied down on the floor at the foot of Tinyanus's bed, but they could not sleep. Titanus filled the void by recalling fond memories— their courtship, the ritual wrestling of her father necessary in order for them to marry, and when Tinyanus was born.

They had been worried then as well. No squid had ever mated with a Veritassian and her physiology as such wouldn't allow for cellular scans. They would know only when the child left the womb. They couldn't have hoped for better. Undersized for a Veritassian baby, but equipped with four back tentacles, the child had the best of both parents, although he still had a minor problem with soaking his pants with bile when he was frightened.

Titanus stood up and ran his hand across the sheets. The bed was dry. Whoever had kidnapped his consciousness was at least kind enough not to torture a child.

They will still have to die, thought Titanus.

A voice called out from the living room. It was Craxx.

"In here, friend."

Craxx walked up to the doorway and stopped. "I heard about Tiny. Is he ok?"

"Where were you? I know you could never have stopped them, but I was counting on you all the same."

"I was here." Craxx looked down the hall, then back to Titanus. He was sweating profusely, and for someone with scaled skin, that was extraordinarily odd.

Titanus raised an arm to reassure his friend with a pat on the shoulder, but Craxx flinched and pulled away.

"You don't look well," said Titanus.

"I'm not. Look, I got something to tell you and you ain't going to like it. I know we've been friends for a long time but I haven't been completely honest with you. I've been working with the rebels."

"In all the time I have known you, you have never discussed politics. How can this be? You aren't able to not speak your mind." He rubbed his head with two hands.

"I know, right? I wanted to so many times. I just jammed a spike into my balls every time I thought I was going to spill the beans! My balls totally leak now. It's a bummer. I've got them all taped up. It's a total scene downstairs."

Titanus sighed. Still Craxx. He was amusing but he would still have to kill him.

"Anyway, balls later. Here's the deal big guy. You're the Emperor's boy now and that pleases us rebels a whole lot. This idea of a 'Citizen's Champion' is a total crock. No one knows what this title is supposed to mean.   And it's clear by how often you have put your foot in your mouth this last week you don't either. You're really just a mascot for the evil empire."

"I am not a mascot. I am a noble man." He began to feel the need to enlarge his fists.

Craxx knew his prideful ways. "Slow down, pal. That ain't gonna solve this. This mascot thing, it's good. Real good, because we have a plot twist for you. The Intergalactic Gladiatorial SkullCrushFest is about to start, and we want you to enter it. The Emperor will get a fucking boner over this, because face it, you are a complete badass and you got a shot."

"I only fight for what's right."

"Well, you're gonna fight for what's right now, friend." Craxx pointed to Tinyanus. "Me and the other rebels called up those Dream Leeches and we want you in the tournament."

"There are some real shitheads fighting this year. Big bounty on their heads. The rebellion needs the cash, so we made arrangements. Think of yourself as a man representing the Emperor who is actually fighting for the rebels but at the end of the day is really just a hitman. You don't need to join the cause. Just kill. And I promise Galactic Credits for kills. Get the kills, get some cheddar, and we set Tinyanus free."

Tinyanus looked peaceful in his Deep Sleep. Where are you now, son? "Is he ok?"

"More than ok," said Craxx. "I love the shit out of your kid. I'd never let him come to harm. Right now he thinks he's at an amusement planet with you and the wife. He's having a blast. I just knew that we'd never convince you to do this unless something serious was at stake."

"You are correct. This is a duplicitous plan you have dragged my family into. I will fight, but not for you, but for them." Titanus picked up Hiediiee. A slick squirt of disgust splashed out from her aimed for his once friend. Putting another hand on his son's forehead, he looked directly into Craxx's eyes.

"And when it is all over, I will kill you as well."

A foul smell filled the room. Craxx apologized and went to find a towel to wipe his loose stool off the floor.

CHAPTER SIX

New gladiators were required to train prior to the tournament. Titanus made the quick trip to the nearest arena planet, not knowing what he would find there. It was a dump. Literally.

Waste Deployment Station 1201 had been a planet-size landfill for three centuries. Here, the garbage of twelve systems was collected and forgotten. A brutal landscape of nothing but old appliances, diapers, fossilized food, RV campers, batteries, unsold books, defecate, and everyone's favorite, radioactive waste, covered the land creating a mountain range of debris and detritus. The clouds cried acid rain continuously and the heat mercilessly trapped the pervasive and pungent stink of rotting death, offering no reprieve. Deep in the middle a sea of plastic and rusting steel, an arena had been carved out from the piles of garbage and it was here that Titanus learned how to kill for sport.

The first business was rest and he found that his sleeping pod had room for four, although only one bed was large enough for his broad frame. A thin, winged woman lay in it, curled up in a fetal position. Titanus tapped her on the shoulder.

She grunted in protest. Without opening her eyes she spoke. "What do you want?"

"The bed. The others are too small."

She sat up, but took her time doing it. She rubbed her eyes. "Hmm."

"Not to displace a lady. My apologies. I will need my proper rest."

"I'm not female."

Titanus set his bag on the floor. Insects skittered to the walls and disappeared into the corners.

"Nor male, nor nothing else. I just am," she said. With a flick of her wings, she took the top bunk. "I'll let you have the bed. One day, soon enough, you'll be at the end of my spear. Name?"

Sitting on the edge of the bunk, he began to unpack his bag. "Titanus."

"Gleedrial the Lucky," she sighed as she inspected her long, sharp fingernails.

"Planet?"

"Not from a planet. From a plane. Not this one either." She stretched her wings out, full spread. She gave a quick ruffle of the feathers and then closed them.

Titanus had his meager clothing neatly folded and set to the end of the bed. "I do not know your race. Your wings look useful."

"Whoopdey do, my man, whoopdey do." She signed once more, fully exaggerating the sound for effect. "So bored. Ready to fight."

"I as well, although I will have much to learn."

"Well, you look tough. Those four arms of yours give you plenty of opportunity to attack. Based on your size and mass, I'd say you are quite strong. Guard your hamstrings. That's the first thing I'd go for."

He ran a hand along the back of his thighs. Good advice.

With a snort she said, "I'd say you have a decent chance. At least for the first several rounds. Much better chance than our roommates. They will be dead in a week."

♦♦♦

An hour later and the door flew open. Laughter filled the room.

"Look Rodrick, we finally have a full house. And he's big as a house. Look at this lout."

Titanus cracked open one eye. It had been a brief but needed nap. Standing over him, two humanoids. One bearded, full plate armor, sword in his hand. The other, thin with long, stringy hair, dressed in a ratty bathrobe.

"Greetings," said Titanus.

Rodrick was the armored one and he seemed inappropriately upbeat for a killer. He held out his off-hand, as his sword was not just being held in his hand, but the hand itself was wrapped in thick bands of leather, as if to prevent him from being disarmed. Distracted, Titanus did not take his hand.

His friend noticed Titanus staring at the sword. "He never lets go of the damn thing. She won't let him."

Rodrick laughed, looking at the sword. "Nope, I can't let her go."

"I am sure that wiping your ass is a challenge," said Titanus.

"Meryzill," said the other, "Magic User Extraordinaire. An absolute pleasure to meet you, you fucking lout. You are hilarious." He paused, stopped by thought. Furrowing his brow, he said, "I know you. You are familiar."

Rodrick used his free hand to play with his beard as he considered the Veritasssian. "He is."

Titanus shrugged.

"I'll remember. You'll see," said Meryzill.

Titanus shrugged again. Movement flickered in the corner of the room, just past the two standing before him. Then it was gone.

"You are both in the tournament?"

"Yes. I fight for my honor and the honor of my fallen kingdom," said Rodrick.

"And I fight because with each life I take, I gain power," said Meryzill as he held his hand out. Delicate blue flames erupted from his palm, then dissipated.

Titanus looked up at Gleedrial. She was in mid-eye roll and she stuck her tongue out at him. "And you?"

She pulled her knees up to her chest. "So I can go home."

Titanus folded both sets of his arms. "I fight for my son."

"I know where I saw you," laughed Meryzill, "You're the guy who jizzed all over that concert. Landed right on top of that no talent singer. You have a massive cock. I have an impressive wand myself."

"Yes, he is the one," Rodrick added. "Most stupendous that was."

"It's big when I need it to be and as big as I need it to be," said Titanus. "Such is an ability of my race."

In the corner, the source of the movement became clear. A fat, hairy spider, easily three feet tall and as wide, began to move to the center of the room. It spoke. "I fight because—"

"Watch this," said Titanus. Crackling with orange electricity, he made a fist and that fist grew five times its normal size. With a deft swing of his arm, he brought the fist down upon the head of the spider. Its exoskeleton shattered, brain and blood showering the room.

Rodrick immediately howled. Meryzill screamed. "No! Jeff! Fuck!" Meryzill fell to his knees and vainly tried to gather the mess, cupping his hands in an attempt to somehow put the spider's cranium back together. "Oh god, oh god, no no no."

Proudly, Titanus stood before them with both sets of arms crossed.

Rodrick lowered his sword and placed its tip delicately on Titanus's chest. "Why did you do that sir? Most dishonorable to kill a man like that."

"It was an insect, what is the harm?"
"That was no insect. That was Jeff. He was our other roommate."
Gleedrial laughed so hard she pissed on her cot.

◆◆◆

The next morning, over a hundred would-be warriors gathered in the yard. There were dozens of relatively standard humanoid warriors, two strangely mutated beaver-men, a talking clam that rode on an hovering platform, cyclopean cheerleaders, a human male underwear model, some kind of fish man with an aquarium helmet, three midgets, and other furry bipeds chattering in a language he could not identify. All of them were heavily armed with recognizable weapons or with devices of unknown purpose.

I packed too lightly, thought Titanus.

From the back, a husky female voice silenced the murmuring crowd of killers and degenerates. "I am Master Instructor Grazina. You will obey my every command or your will die here on this garbage heap. Now line up!"

Standing in the front, Titanus waited as he heard her making her way through the rows, flinging insults, correcting posture, and slapping ass. It was too much to resist taking a peek over his shoulder. She was impressive. Tall, easily seven foot, with broad shoulders that were exaggerated by spiky bronze pauldrons. Her three bodacious breasts were safely protected by a full breastplate, which also featured spikes, making them a serious weapon in close combat. A leather skirt with bronze ringlets completed her armor kit. In her right hand was a mammoth war axe.

A Iguana-like creature, with a cigar stub planted on its lower lip stood to the right of Titanus. "This must be a lot for you to handle, Veritassian," it croaked.

"You do not know me. It would be wise of you not to speak."

"It would be wise of you not to speak," it sneered.

A heavy gauntlet came down on Titanus's shoulder. "Next time, instead of staring at my tits, take a holo. It'll give you something to rub that famous cock to." She took a long look at him, from top to bottom. Then she smiled. "Looks like we have a celebrity here with us, warriors." She positioned Titanus so that he faced the group. "This here, in case some of you live under a rock, which is quite possible, is the first 'Citizen's Champion.' As a citizen, I find that insulting. What do you think?"

There was a little chitter-chatter and then the comments started flying.

"He's a pussy."

"No, a BIG pussy."

"Dude's a fart."

"Looks strong to me."

"Show us your cock, big guy."

"When's lunch?"

Grazina pushed Titanus back into the line. "You are nothing here, Titanus. Nothing until you prove otherwise."

"I had not planned to—"

"DO NOT speak. Now then, take a swing at me."

Titanus did not hesitate. He balled up a fist and let one go. She easily dodged it and, using three fingers, struck a nerve center just under his rib cage, sending a lighting bolt of pain down his left leg. He dropped down to one knee and held his side.

The crowd guffawed.

"Nothing," she said. "You are the champion of nothing."

CHAPTER SEVEN

Combatants were sorted by general fighting style and abilities. Titanus was thrown into a group of meatheads that used pure brawn. Grazina was a intelligent and savvy fighter, they were not. These guys, they didn't look for pressure points or use strategy of any kind. They just did their best to grind their opponent into the ground. Titanus took his licks, delivered many of his own, and earned the general respect of a small group of fighters who were so brain poor they couldn't scrape two thoughts together.

Throughout the arena, a symphony of pain: the pings of crashing metal, the screams of victory and defeat, the crunching of bones. Not everyone would be leaving the training arena alive. It mattered little in a tournament with a thousand fighters to place. There was plenty of room for casualties.

Between sparring rounds, Titanus took a break from the continuous ball-busting of his heavily muscled training partners and found a quiet spot to catch his breath. The intensity of the morning had kept him from taking in the surroundings, which looked like shit, as they were comprised completely with filth and rubbish. Surprisingly they still needed attention. A talking rat, roughly two feet in height and wearing dark blue coveralls approached him. The rat was pulling a car filled with cleaning supplies. A custodian.

"Hey buddy," said the rat. "Got a smoke?"

"I don't smoke. It will kill you."

"Hell, dude. Everything here will kill you. Fucking non-smokers. I spend all day cleaning up blood and brains and you get all high-and-mighty with me. Fucker. Anyway, here's this."

He handed Titanus a note.

"Open it when you are alone. Really alone. Not sitting off on the sidelines of the killing fields. Fucker."

The rat turned and with great stain, pulled the cart around. Titanus didn't get but a moment before there was the sudden flutter of wings overhead. Gleedrial took a seat next to him.

"Why the long face, Tits?"

He pointed to the cart. "Do you see those mops? In that janitor's cart? They remind me of my wife."

"That's fucked up. You some kind of sexist? Cleaning supplies remind you of your wife?"

"No. She is a squid. They kind of look like her."

"Oh."

"My wife, she is a very strong woman. She is at home with my child, who is not well. I could not do what she is doing. She is stronger than me."

Gleedrial ran her hands over his bulging biceps. "I know squids are strong, but I don't think so."

Titanus pointed to his skull. "Stronger here." He pointed to his heart. "Stronger there. I miss her."

"And yet you are here, getting bruises and lacerations, well on your way to more serious wounds."

Gleedrial looked as undamaged as the day before. Her skin was a smooth ceramic. Its color was uniformly eggshell. Her armor and toga had not a dink or dent. "You have not been hurt?" he asked.

"They don't call me 'The Lucky' for nothing, big guy." She sighed. "I'm a ringer. I can't be hurt. I'm here to weed out the weak. They don't make for good viewing. Audiences only want to see the best fight the best."

"Everyone can be hurt. Arrogance leads to mistakes."

An slight electric glow danced from her fingertips, moved up her arms, then out to her wings. "See that? That's what luck looks like. I only have one weakness, one thing that can negate it, and you'll never know. Just pray I'm not in your bracket. Plan to ask for mercy if you are."

And with that, she flew away, punctuating her departure with a shrill war cry. Titanus stood and walked back into the fight.

◆◆◆

He could hear Rodrick and Meryzill through the bathroom door. They were out in the main room, having some laughs, pointing out the minor wounds that they had received. They didn't seem to be taking their training very seriously.

Confident that he wouldn't be disturbed, he unfolded the paper the rat janitor had given him. It was from Craxx. It read:

Hey Tits, how's it hanging? KILL anybody with that cock of yours yet? Just wanted to let you know that everything is fine on the home front. Your wife and son are in no danger. You don't have to worry. I am still your friend, even if you might hate me right now. I'll spare you the boring details for now, but it's very important that you make a strong impression over the next few days. The media is buzzing, and we can't have you getting whacked before the games start. If you have anything to say to Hiediiee or Tiny, just pass a note onto the rat and I will pass it on to THEM. That's ALL for now.

Craxx.

(P.S.) I always really liked you and I'd like to not be dead when this is all over. Think about it!

On the bottom of the page, there was a small stain. Titanus brought the paper up to his nose and sniffed. It was a message from Hiediiee. It was the scent of reassurance. It smelled like love. She must have dripped on the note when Craxx wasn't looking! This bit of brilliance gave him a small amount of comfort, which was interrupted by Meryzill, who came flying into the bathroom. His robe was flapping, and for a brief moment, Titanus could see that his flesh was covered in boils.

Boils that blinked.

Not boils, but eyes.

Hundreds of them.

"Gotta drain the wand," he muttered.

His sudden entrance threw Titanus off balance and he began to fall backwards out into the main room. Trying to stabilize his body, he increased the size of his back leg and foot, not knowing that directly behind him, Rodrick had lied down to take a nap. His sword arm dangled from the bunk and its placement was in the path of Titanus's mighty foot, which came down upon it with great force.

There was the sound of tearing flesh as Rodrick's arm was pulled from its socket and Titanus felt the gush of hot blood upon his back; his ears were filled with the screams of the now amputated knight. The slick blood caused Titanus to fall, the sword sticking out between his legs, pointing to the ceiling, a metal erection. Rodrick rolled off his bunk onto the floor and fell next to him.

"Why?" he asked, his face white with horror. "Why didn't you look first, you clumsy oaf?" The floor disappeared under the torrent of blood. But before Titanus could react, Meryzill flew out of the bathroom with a fireball at the ready.

"You are too dangerous to live, my friend. You did this on purpose," the magic user said, running full speed across the room.

He ran too fast and didn't notice the pool of blood on the floor. His bathrobe, just an inch too long, was caught underfoot and with that, he slipped onto Rodricks's sword. He muttered curses as he slid down the blade. The fireball vanished in his hand.

"Son of a bitch. You are smarter than you look," he said with dying breath.

Titanus felt a rush of guilt, but it soon passed. Perhaps now he would be able to get some sleep, without all of the late night gossip and lame ghost stories Rodrick and Meryzill seemed to adore sharing.

He took a shower to wash off the mage's blood. He felt better afterwards.

CHAPTER EIGHT

It was a night filled with torments. Fitful, sweaty sleep populated by fervent dreams, nightmares, and a woman's voice that he could not place. Images of Dream Leeches, his dear wife, pools of blood, and his son's face shifted on and off the stage of his dream consciousness, and the carnival of dreadnight was punctuated by a waking nightmare in which his cock grew so large it blotted out the sun and poked a moon in its eye.

The voice, the dream woman, begged him to take her into his arms. Hold me tight, she whispered repeatedly. Take me. He ran down halls and stairs chasing this voice, but he could not find her. Only the brief glimpse of white, flowing robes and flitting hair. Then mist. Then he stood at a lake. Its water was dead still, a perfect mirror that reflected the stars in the sky above.

He woke suddenly, the butt end of Gleedrial's spear tapping on his forehead. "Get up fucker, it's the big day."

He sat up in bed and stretched all four of his arms to their full, but standard extension. He cracked his neck. He ripped an epic fart. He scratched his belly and released a tremendous yawn from the confines of his lungs.

"Well that was the worst fucking night I have had since," he said. Looking up, he caught her mid-undress. Her lack of genitalia was moderately disturbing but strangely expected.

"Same. That fucking bitch wouldn't shut up."

Titanus's ears perked. "You heard her as well. I assumed it was a dream."

"Nope." Gleedrial pointed to Rodrick's sword. The cleaning rats had left it where it lay. "That's the bitch."

"That is a sword."

"Much more than that, star sailor."

Titanus walked to it and kneeled. It was quite beautiful. Gleaming. Perfect, with not a single mark or ding in the metal. Deeply etched letters of some unknown language ran down the length of its blade. He reached out. It begged to be touched.

Gleedrial's hand clamped down on his wrist. "Don't, unless you want it to be a permanent part of your ensemble. The bitch is alive in there, but she needs a host."

Titanus stood and took a step back. Then another for good measure. "Curious."

"That's a word. You're a goddamn poet."

The yard was filled with the sounds that had become second nature to Titanus. The clang and clank of metal, guttural macho sounds of exertion, the occasional cry for mercy. But when he took to the field and began his morning stretches and calisthenics, it fell into silence. Still air, followed by the low mutterings of his fellow warriors. Then some pointing and a few unintelligible jeers.

Then mean-spirited taunts. But there were a few cheers as well.

"Way to go, big red. Killed your own fucking roommates."

"What an asshole."

"That's the stuff!"

"Surprised he didn't kill himself by accident too."

"Dumbass!"

"Whom are we talking about?"

"You're my hero, Mr. Titanus."

They are just trying to distract me. Take me off my game. It's just trash talk. Ignore them.

But it was impossible to ignore them, especially after a respectably sized group performed a complex choreographed musical number devoted to his clumsiness. In addition to a series of highly technical and well-executed dance moves, the show included fireworks and a floating sperm whale that could hit a falsetto that was so far beyond recorded range that it created a portal to a dimension filled with floating cubes of plasma. Or cheese. It was hard to tell the difference as the gate closed as quickly as it opened.

A line formed in front of him, but he did his best to complete a set of sit-ups. Clutching wads of paper, most of them wanted autographs. Handshakes. Some held out their asses and begged for a football pat. "At least cup it," they begged. They all had questions. They all wanted to be his new best friend. A second group gathered in a corner to show their disapproval for his methods.

Perplexed, Titanus attempted to explain the events that happened the night before. He presented the truth behind the death of his roommates and his regret for not having eliminated them in combat. They were not interested in hearing a sincere explanation and interrupted him with banal questions or stuttered greetings.

A fat flying insectoid began to weave its way through the line, cutting past the throngs of sweaty killers. "Out of my way, you mongrels. Out of my way!" He bounced about, rather than flying, his pudginess making him a bit too heavy for his smallish wings. He had no qualms about using the heads, shoulders, and faces of the crowd to propel himself towards Titanus.

With a cigar chomping grin, he held out an appendage in greeting. "Hello, you big galoot. I'm Methll Bertbrae. I'll be your coach for the games."

Later on, when Titanus shared the news of his new coach with Gleedrial, she was deeply impressed.

"Methil? He's the real deal," she said.

CHAPTER NINE

Methil brought order to the chaos of the last week. A coach with years of experience, he was on the tail end of a hall-of-fame career, but it had been some time since he had coached a winner. Titanus had caught his eye. He was currently evaluating how much work was ahead for them both.

"I like your instincts, Tits. You have a natural ability to see the field," he offered, buzzing about as Titanus pummeled a training dummy into submission. "Having four arms is a plus." Methil scribbled something in a notebook. "Very tall."

Titanus continued to hammer on the dummy, doing his best not to be distracted by the high-pitched hum of Methil's undersized wings.

"Good concentration. Solid stance."

Methil's positive comments gave Titanus a boost. He fired a quick salvo of jabs and prepared to land a final haymaker. Delirious, the dummy waved for mercy.

"Please sir, I have a doll and two action figures at home. I can't take anymore."

Titanus raised his fists. "I beg of you. I just got them a new play set. They haven't even seen it yet."

Titanus gave it a grunt and untied it. "Very well. Go to them."

Methil flew over. "Good work, Tits. Now this cock of yours? Is it the only thing that grows? I know some Veritassians are more gifted than others."

"I can enlarge any body part I wish."

"That's good. They will most likely look to the cock. You can surprise them." He handed Titanus a towel. "No one gets to see who they fight before the fight. It's all random. But your cock is known across many galaxies, and with this 'Champion' business, most fighters will have your number from Jump Street."

Methil sat Titanus down and explained the critical need for surprise. Titanus listened. There would be no pre-game tape or strategy sessions. No way to know what abilities the opponent would have.

"But I've been coaching for a fucking long time," said Methil. He puffed his cigar. "I can tell you what to do seconds after I see the poor bastard. Nobody's been coaching gladiators for as long as I have. Losers kill their coaches."

"Have you not had losing fighters?"

"Sure, but I used to be able to fly a lot faster. They couldn't catch me. Now, those days are done. I'm going to retire. You'll be my last fighter and you are going to win. I'll make you a legend and I'll go out on top."

◆◆◆

Soon all the fighters had coaches and were moved from their pods to a series of shacks that lined the outer edge of the arena grounds. Titanus had not seen Gleedrial in parting. Although he couldn't respect her misanthropic thinking, she had provided a feminine essence that had made the absence of his wife just slightly more bearable.

Methil didn't give him a chance to think about her for long. He was too busy explaining the finer aspects of the games—the constant distraction of the media, the corporate sponsorships, the arbitrary changes in rules, and the random selection of both location and opponent. Just as every challenger would be an unknown, so would be the location of the fight. Each fight was hosted by a different planet, and with so many fighters entered in the tournament, the amount of variables was so overwhelming that it was much easier not to prepare at all.

Methil's advice was simple. "You'll just have to stay frosty. You're the goddamn 'Citizen's Champion' and everyone is going to want a piece of your ass."

On the final night of training, Titanus received a gift basket from the Emperor. In it was a bar of chocolate, a teddy bear, candied almonds, and a small jewelry box that he could not open. The card read, Make me proud. Methil ate the almonds, Titanus the chocolate. The bear went in his bag, an eventual gift for Tinyanus. The box would have to be bothered with later—or maybe not at all.

Although rest was imperative, there would be no sleep. Tradition demanded that all of the fighters participate in a press conference/fashion show and dissenters would be, at the very least, skewered on the popular Fashion Critique Squawk-show, "What the FUCK are you Wearing?" as well as twelve billion fashion blogs.

There was little complaint from the gladiators. The arena could kill you, but the possibility of getting torn apart on WTFRUW was truly terrifying. That show was brutal.

CHAPTER TEN

Grazina was not only an experienced trainer, but she was an expert stage manager as well. The morning had been brutal; the fittings, makeup, and last minute touches had people running but Grazina kept them organized. Whiny designers were immediately flogged and the media were kept in iron cages to prevent them from sneaking backstage. Grazina had a heartwarming way of using the word "maggot" that took away the obvious insult. She had even taken the time to give Titanus a few encouraging words.

"You have a great chance of not dying as long as you aren't completely stupid," she had said.

You weren't going to get anything better out of her; she had beaten five hopeful gladiators to death the day before. Their offense was cutting the line to the showers. She had very little wiggle room when it came to the rules.

Titanus had been assigned a kit of simple bronze armor pieces and two square, plain iron hammers. The armor covered his forearms, shins, shoulders, and crotch. A cape was thrown in a for a bit of panache. Grazina smacked his bare red ass and sent him up to the runway. The whole thing seemed preposterous. A complete and utter denial of the truth of the games, which was to kill and kill well.

"You're going to get some fool notions today," warned Methil. "You will want to say something stupid, because it's stupid. You will have to fight your nature."

"I can only say what I think or feel, so I will not speak at all," Titanus had responded.

"Do that for as long as you can."

Titanus lasted about three minutes before his bluntness pissed off a three-headed Ferubinite photojournalist, one of the hosts of "What the FUCK are you Wearing," and a small contingent of religious protestors. Apparently no one thought highly of being told that their questions represented a new strain of brainlessness or the suggestion that their existence could end moments after their refusal to make way. Immediate reports from the show named the "Citizen's Champion" the

"Citizen's Cunt," the "Citizen's Douchebag," and simply "asshole." Only the Veritassian media contingent praised him for his appropriate assessment of the scene, even though they were the first to be told to "fuck straight off."

◆◆◆

After two hours of parading up and down the runway with all of the other warriors, Titanus finally took his seat at the press table. Most of the fighters had one or two reporters sticking various sensors and recorders in their faces, but with his tentative fame, Titanus and his famous coach were forced to face an onslaught of blank faces and moronic questions.

Methil knew how to talk shit. Titanus had caught his eye, he explained, due to the tremendous effort and strength he displayed in the training arena. When Titanus began to explain how he accidentally killed his roommates, Methil flew in front of his face and planted his beefy bug butt directly into Titanus's mouth. When other questions arose regarding his role as "Citizen's Champion," Methil went as far as jamming his stinger into Titanus's tongue to get him from revealing how bogus the title really was. When asked what he thought his fighter's chances were in the months ahead, Methil feigned offense, as if such a question was a direct insult to his intelligence.

After being stung about eight times, Titanus's tongue was so swollen he couldn't speak. At this point, Methil allowed him to take questions, peppering him with small smacks on the head when it looked like a muffled response might actually be translated.

It was critical to get things rolling in the right direction. The crowd of camera drones, self-aware camerabots, holorecorders, cluster microphone bombs, and snarling coke-fueled living reporters assured that every word, every movement, every facial expression that the coach and the fighter made would be instantly recorded and broadcast across the universe. No doubt everyone was watching, from the Emperor to the kidnapping rebels. Titanus learned quickly that he would not only have to fight his way through the tournament, but he would have to fight his very nature as well. Gladiators that became unpopular with the media quickly disappeared from the public viewing eye and as Methil explained, "Got assigned shit fights and suicide missions." In short, there would be no rise to the top for those who didn't dance with the media, and they were fickle bitches.

Eventually the questions subsided. Titanus took a breath. "Wellth, howth didth Ith doth, coach?"

"I've had shits that smelled better," said Methil.

Titanus winced. "Thath badth?"

"You can't help it, Tits. Speaking of, did you notice that reporter with the six tits? Holy fuck, I'd like to motorboat that business." Methil blew a thick cloud of cigar smoke.

"Indeedth."

Methil flew up to his ear. "Now, there's just one little bit and then we can get going, ok? For the next five minutes all I want you to think about is how you are going to tear ass through the tournament. Think bloody fucking victory. Think triumph. Think champion."

Titanus closed his eyes and tried to focus his thoughts.

"You don't have to shut your lids, dumb ass. Just think!"

Titanus opened his eyes to find three hooded figures standing in front of the table. In unison, they removed their hoods. Bald, humanoid and sexless, the three pale skinned figures said nothing. They simply stared directly at Titanus.

Methil patted him on the back. "Remember what I said and try not to move. Just five quick minutes."

It was a five-minute eternity. Much like the time he and his wife waited for Tinyanus to recite his lines in a school play about the Nemonian Sex Slaves and their fight for reasonably nutritious cafeteria food. Tinyanus had put too many dramatic pauses in his delivery that day and theater critics had been merciless in their evaluation of the second grade of Quadrant Four Elementary School and their lack of any true acting talent. After the show, he spent an hour with his head in his wife's crotch. She happily returned the favor.

At the end of the five minutes, Methil whispered once more into Titanus's ear. "Now get ready for the freak-out."

The three beings looked to one another and nodded. With smiles suggesting they were pleased with their effort, they held hands and formed a triangle. They began to chant. The language was unknown and it was a deep, guttural sound that came from them. A glowing ball of energized plasma formed in the middle of their triangle, growing as they increased the volume of their chants.

"Uh, Methil?"

"Don't worry, kid. It's safe."

The crackling sphere of energy overtook their bodies and they exploded into flames; they became ashes in an instant.

"Lumins," said Methil. "Ever heard of them?"

"No. Is that normal?"

"Quite," said Methil, landing on the table. "They record an event into memory. The stress of it causes them to spontaneously combust."

"What's the point? It is a waste."

Methil scratched his belly and straightened out his necktie. "Their memory of the recorded event enters the mass subconscious and from that point forward, everyone across the universe just kind of remembers it."

"So that's why I had to get it right?"

"Yep. Otherwise people would remember the wrong thing."

Immediately Titanus began to worry. He had not followed Methil's advice at all.

◆◆◆

After the fuckadilly circus that was the fashion show, Titanus was finally shown mercy and allowed to return to his quarters. The final stage of gladiator school was now complete. They'd be on a transport first thing in the morning and his debut fight would be a day later.

"Just a pinch of time to screw that head on straight, you big red cock-knocker," Methil said as he slapped Titanus on the shoulder. "If you need me, I'll be at the only strip club on this literal dung heap. I'll be the drunkest motherfucker there."

The shack felt painfully empty. Titanus reclined on his ill-fitting cot and practiced the few mediation techniques he knew—deep breathing and a quick jerk. The breathing did little, but a solid nut bust later and he could feel sweet sleep approaching.

There was a quiet knock on the door.

Too tired to get up, Titanus beckoned the knocker to enter; he recognized his visitor as one of the feral beaver men from the first day of gladiator school. The beaver, fur ruffled and unkempt, could have used a trim. The exhausted Titanus couldn't muster the energy to inform him.

The beaver spoke with a wheeze. "Hhheey, sir. Just a moment of your time, pluhhlese."

Titanus sighed. "Yes."

"I represent the fuh-fine fun-folks who pu-put you huh-here," said the beaver. "The ru-rebels, huh."

The beaver began to pace the room. He was clearly trying to keep some distance between Titanus and himself. "I highm just the messenger, heeeesh. Don't get up. Huh."

50

Titanus took some consolation in knowing that he could quickly crush the varmint's skull.

"Fine. Go on."

"You-who ha-have the note, yeh-yes? From yah-your friend?" The beaver made bizarre gestures with his hands.

"Did you-hoooo understandth?"

"My family is safe. Is this true?"

The beaver nodded excitedly. "The th-second part is more important-th. It-th was th-thought th-that you-th wouldn't get-th it."

The beaver's wheeze was unbearable. Titanus wished to enlarge one of his feet and squash him where he stood.

"Fucking tell me and get out. Your mere existence tries me, beaver."

"In-th th-the fights-ths, you-th will be given-th a choice." The beaver began to cough over his words. "But-th, ack ack, you-th muthst never spare-th th-them."

"Don't spare any of my opponents?"

"Kill them! Destroy them! Leave nothing but entrails and weeping widows! Every warrior you face will be an enemy of the cause. They all must die! Do this and everything will work out."

The beaver's eyes widened. "Hey, I think I finally got that hair out of my throat. Getting beaver hair stuck in your throat is the worst."

"Anything else?"

The beaver shook his head. "Nope."

"Then get the fuck out."

The beaver left and Titanus attempted sleep once more, but to no avail.

A lyrical voice floated out from the corner of the room. Rodrick's sword. It sang to him.

"Please, shut up. Let a man sleep."

"I thought you might like a lullaby," it complained.

"Fuck off."

"Do you want to hold me?"

"Fuck off. Let me sleep."

"Would you like to hear my origin story?"

"Fuck the fuck off, you piece of shit metal toothpick!"

Titanus turned over and covered his ears with a pillow, but he could still hear her voice inside his head. She prattled on endlessly about ancient and dead empires on distant planets, heroes and gods, and her killer salsa recipe. She sang a ballad, read him a poem, and repeatedly asked him to hold her. She promised gifts and powers beyond his experience. All she heard in return was:

"Fuck off."

Eventually she did wear him down and convinced him to place her in his duffle bag. "Perhaps tomorrow or the next," she said, "you will make me yours."

"Whatever," he said, "as long as you shut the fuck up for a while."

CHAPTER ELEVEN

In five hundred arenas on five hundred planets scattered across the universal grid, one thousand warriors waited in their green rooms. The first day of fighting was about to begin. Titanus, unproven yet confident, was getting a pre-fight pep talk.

It was classic Methil Bertbrae.

"Just get in there and crush the sonuvabitch. Really grind him from the get-go. No stops."

Methil wasn't too big on strategy, but it had served him well over the years, enough to get the Hall of Fame talk buzzing. He just needed one final champion and that guy was sitting in front of him, putting a thin coat of Vaseline over his entire body. Methil could barely contain his excitement.

"It'll keep you from bleeding too much," Methil advised.

High above Atacama III, Prax Stiverson and Blatt Blatzz were running down the tale of the tape.

"We all know Titanus as the man with the cock that could, Blatt, but there isn't much to tell us that he has, if you will excuse the pun, a fighting chance," said Prax, the most popular sports analyst in in cross-dimensional sports broadcasting. Although he was only a brain floating in a jar of green vicious fluid, he had an eye for the game.

"Very true, Prax," said Blatt. "We don't know much about the Veritassian other than he knows where to put his dick."

"And that's why, fight fans, you'll be getting exclusive coverage of Titanus's fights by the two of us, throughout the tournament. The Emperor demanded nothing less that the best in media professionalism for—"

"The 'Citizen's Champion'—whatever that means," finished Blatt.

Below their broadcasting platform, the crowd frothed with excitement. The grandness of the spectacle was unmatched and for a lowly desert planet such as Atacama III, the chance to host a fight at any level was a great honor. The locals, a race of centaurs featuring scorpion bodies with humanoid torsos and arms, packed the house. The skitter and clicking of their claws filled the air with the sound of a million salad tongs opening and closing.

"The crowd is certainly worked up," said Blatt. "There's never been a fight here before and they are good and ready."

"To be fair, there's never been a reason to have a fight here before. They have only had a written language for about three months," added Prax.

"Seems a bit condescending."

"Hey, I only read what's on the teleprompter."

"You're a brain in a jar. How the fuck do you read anything?"

"Can we just move on?"

"Sure, right after you tell me how you can read the teleprompter. Must be magic," said Blatt with a sneer. To be fair, there was little that he could say that Blatt wouldn't challenge. His contentious color analyst worked from a deep pit of envy. Prax got laid a lot more than he did, and coming from a race where males had five penises, Blatt didn't have any excuse. His pants, however, did fit like a glove.

"No time! But what it is time for?" Prax expertly deflected, "It's time for the taste of the Old World with Auntie Nuke's Quantum Pasta. So delicious, and the food is immediately transported to one of your duplicates in an alternate timeline, so you never get fat and you can eat as much as you want!"

"What happens to the alternate version of you? Do they get fat?" asked Blatt.

"That's the best part. Who cares? Let them get fat. All the eating, none of the guilt. Auntie Nuke's Quantum Pasta. Replicate some in your home today!"

♦♦♦

Methil flew about, circling Titanus. He chomped down on his cigar. "Anytime now, that iron gate is going to open up in front of you. Now look kid, we have no idea what is going to come out of that door on the other side. You have to be ready for anything. The main goal here is to last the first round. By then I will have a good idea on what the fuck to do, if you haven't figured it out already. Just get through the first round. That's all you have to do."

"I will do that."

"That's good. Think about whatever it was that brought you here. You haven't told me, but I know that it wasn't that damn fool Emperor. There's something that has been hiding in the back of that thick skull of yours since we met. Keep that close and you'll get through it.

Titanus could feel his body swell. Every cell pushing its limit, testing the edge of its membrane. His body ached to expand, to enlarge. His heart pumped, rapid pistons generating an abundance of power. His fists, all four, clenched and grew a quarter size larger.

The klaxonbot could be heard hovering just outside the door, moving about the arena. It began to sound its horn. Titanus drew a deep breath and held it. Methil slapped a simple iron helm down on his head.

"That's the stuff. Go crack some skulls, kid."

The gate slowly pulled up and away. The bright suns of Atacama III blasted into the access tunnel, bathing it in blinding light. Titanus put his head down and ran out to meet his foe. Across the desert floor, an shambling mound came forward, moaning.

"Oh my," said Blatt. "Titanus has pulled a tough card for his first fight."

"Hoary Muggottth? Yeah, they are the worst! Let's see what the Veritassian can do!"

Titanus slowed to a jog but continued to move toward the center of the arena. The crowd howled, screamed, and clacked their claws. A million tiny cameradrones flittered about, all fighting for the best angle to capture the fight. An announcer's voice boomed from the multitude of speakers that clung to every free rail and surface in the arena that wasn't already occupied by a holomonitor or animated billboard. "Let the SkullCrushFest begin!"

He considered his opponent, a moving pile of moss and mold, branches, leaves, and vines. It smelled of compost; its pungent scent was of dung and decay. It dragged its form across the sand, sending up small puffs of dust behind it. The surface of the beast moved and wriggled about, as if it was made of many smaller living creatures. A complete ecosystem, held together by a single, communal consciousness.

It made the first charge, expelling a noxious gas as it moved forward with surprising speed. Titanus leapt to his left, dodging it easily and responded with a short jab to the back of what he assumed was its head. The moment his banded knuckles stuck the creature, he knew he had miscalculated. His fist, down to the wrist, was pulled into the mound. The burning acid bite of its toxic secretions clung to Titanus's skin. His arm muscles twitched in agony.

"Motherfucker!" said Titanus.

"Get it out of there before you lose it!" Methil screamed.

Titanus had never heard a pile of mold laugh before. It was awkward and unnatural. The Muggottth taunted him, pulling away slightly to create suction and draw in more of his arm.

Up top, Prax and Blatt frantically listed every possible strategy that Titanus could employ in this moment. It was easy for them; they weren't currently feeling their flesh burning away.

"That's gotta hurt," said Blatt. "Can't touch a Muggottth. Didn't his mother ever teach him that?"

"I know what your mother taught me, Prax. Remind me to tell you after the fight."

"Stay off moms, dude."

"Ok. I'll get off yours as soon as I've finished."

"Fucking guy."

The Muggottth continued to go to work on Titanus's arm. He could feel thousands of small needle-like appendages attempting to pierce his skin. The acid might caused extreme pain, but it would take more than a forest of tiny teeth to pierce his tough Veritassian hide.

He fell to one knee, questioning how much longer he could endure the torment. The green mound began to shift, making itself alternatively taller and thinner, then shorter and squat.

This thing is fucking trying to chew up my arm. Have to do something about this.

Over the roar of the bloodthirsty throngs of Atacamans, he could hear Methil screaming.

"Punch it in the mind, you fucker. RIGHT IN THE MIND!"

He couldn't mean to punch it again. His seasoned coach continued to motion for him to lay some knuckles.

To punch or not to punch?

Methil continued to scream, his face becoming a deep red color. "PUNCH HIM AGAIN, DUMBASS!"

Shrugging, Titanus rolled up his three remaining fists and fired them into the shambling mass of the Muggottth. Now Titanus had all four of his limbs deep inside and once again, the Muggottth attacked with its toxic bile, coating Titanus's flesh with its organic napalm.

"NOW FINISH HIM! ENLARGE!"

There was a roar of thunder and a burst of fiery orange lightning as Titanus enlarged all four of his fists simultaneously, driving them deeper within the creature. When he felt his knuckles bump, he lifted up with a sudden jerk, pulling the Muggottth over his head, falling backwards as he drove the foul monstrosity into the earth; the collision caused it to rupture into hundreds of smaller globs of green goo and growth.

There was another crackle and pop of energy as Titanus rose and increased the size of his feet. He stomped down on the fragmented Muggottth, grinding each bit he could find deep into the earth. Its only defense system against the assault was a cloud of nagging, biting insects that did little to distract Titanus from dancing his way to victory.

When the klaxonbot signaled the end of the first round, Titanus was covered in burns, boils, and goo, but there wasn't much Muggottth left to fight. He couldn't help but sprout a big, sloppy grin.

◆◆◆

Methil buzzed from burn to burn, applying a salve that instantly removed the residual pain from the Muggottth's bile.

"Didn't do much damage. You got tough skin. Makin' a note of that."

Titanus sat on a small bench on the edge of the arena near the gate he had used to enter it. The crowd seemed very pleased by his first round performance. The Muggottth was attempting to gather itself back into a mound, but there wasn't much for it to work with.

"Ok, Tits. Here's the deal. You got this guy, it's just a matter of going out, doing a bit of dance and then ending the thing. You'll have to trade blows and whatnot." He applied a goo to Titanus's fingertips. They felt cool and baby smooth.

"Then you'll get a moment to decide to kill him or spare him. You should probably spare him. It will make you look honorable. Makes for a more pleasant after-party as well. People won't tiptoe around you, scared you'll snap their neck if they eat too much cheese dip."

The note had read: KILL THEM ALL.

I guess they'll just have to stick to the crudité.

The klaxonbot swooped in for a dramatic circle around the arena and sounded its siren. The arena exploded with the sound of rabid Atacamans.

"Listen to this crowd, Prax, they are loving it!" said Blatt.

Prax bobbed up and down within his jar with gusto. "There's no denying, those claws make a clatter that could give a Nebuilian Narwhal a brain aneurysm. Or, in layman's terms, it's a sound that makes one want to drive a spike in their auditory nerve sacs."

Down on the arena floor, The Muggottth did not approach Titanus but rather moved away from him.

"Well Prax, turns out that mossy mound is a real pussy."

His brain-in-a-jar partner understood the joke but chose to ignore it; he enjoyed being a dick like that sometimes.

Titanus approached the Muggottth, increasing the size of his feet with every step. The arena screamed for him to dispatch the monstrosity, and he marched with singular purpose. He closed the distance, ready to crush his first opponent and end the fight. The Muggottth was shuddering in fear, clearly subjugating itself. It wanted mercy.

"Remember what I told ya," Methil barked.

Remember the note, thought Titanus. Remember Tinyanus, trapped by Dream Leeches while Hiediiee sits vigil by his side.

By the rail there was a decorative planter filled with colorful and exotic flowers that spread a scent of pure vanilla and freshly washed puppies. It was there that Titanus ignored the calls for mercy he heard from the crowd as he squashed what was left of the Muggottth out of existence. He did not know that in the planter were the Muggottth's wife, children, and extended family. As their father was obliterated, they began to wilt and wither.

Prax noted the carnage and made a quip about a vegetarian's dilemma. Blatt dismissed him for being moderately insensitive, but would later show his true colors when he stuck what was left of the plant creature into a three-foot bong and smoked it. There really isn't a greater high than Muggottth weed.

That night, Titanus slept well. One down, with an unknown number to go. In his dreams, he had a tea party with Rodrick's sword and something funny happened in his codpiece.

CHAPTER TWELVE

Peepantz was one of five large moons that orbited a gas giant. It was the finest day care satellite in its sector. Wealthy parents from twelve different systems used it to kennel their young, often dropping them off for long periods of time. Every once in a while, someone would "conveniently" abandon his or her progeny there for life. These malcontents became the guards; they immediately used their wards as punching bags to purge their frustrations. The only solace new inmates could take was that upon an individual's eighteenth birthday, they were given a party hat, a cake and a public execution. As such, bullies had limited time to practice their dark arts. This vicious cycle of abuse had been going on for centuries.

Appropriately, the mob that filled PleyPlaice Field was angst-filled, indignant, and relentlessly horny. They had bad skin and body image issues. Their taste in music was terrible. There was nothing you could say to them that wouldn't be met with a sneer. It would be here that Titanus would fight his second opponent.

Methil surveyed the crowd. "Lotta fine young ass out there."

Titanus tried to ignore him.

"Tight cheeks."

Titanus began to strap on his armor. The Muggottth's juices had stripped its gleam but it was still structurally intact.

"Tight fucking cheeks. You know, legal age is a completely different concept for insectoids, right? I'm not pervvin' out. It's legit for me."

"Right." Titanus polished his helmet and armor.

Methil closed the viewing slot. "Just trying to lighten the mood. Yeah, that's it."

"What's the field look like?"

"All business. That's what I like about you, Tits. Field is rectangular in shape. Filled with playground crap like flaying wheels, scraper slides, ball pens, and crotch-pinching swings. Opponent comes out the opposite end as usual. Longer field here. You'll have more distance to size him up."

Methil gulped down a cup of coffee and looked down at his clipboard. "You ranked much higher for this round. A lot of people watching. You'll pull a tough motherfucker for this fight."

◆◆◆

Prax and Blatt flew their broadcast dais throughout the crowd. They were grabbing a few tasty bits of crowd color.

"Thanks for joining us high above PleyPlaice Field! I'm Prax Stiverson!"

"And I'm Blatt Blatzz. We have a hell of fight for you today. The once untested now confirmed Badass of Veritassia, Titanus versus—" Blatt scrambled through his notes. 'Some other dude."

A quick flash of electricity ran through Prax's brain jar. It was the color of wince.

"Classic Blatt. You are such a wanker."

The broadcast dais zipped along. The savage youth that filled the seats did their best to take the platform out with a variety of small caliber weapons and Molotov cocktails. Others acted annoyed and huffed by the obvious pandering.

Still, when the camera drones captured them for the jumbo holomonitor scoreboard, they jumped up and down, flashing gang signs while shaking their asses. There were also a few obligatory titties, which pleased Methil considerably. As soon as the camera drones moved away, they returned the heavy chips to their shoulders.

Blatt swung his microphone around and stumbled upon a young female Wallie, a short and stout race known for being so cute merely looking at it caused cancer in laboratory biological specimens. He tried not to stare directly into her large, spherical eyes.

"What do you think, sweetie?" Blatt attempted to pull back but found he could not.

Prax commanded the dais to move up and out. It struggled to move, caught in her cuteness field. His brain jar was lined with protective material but his friend was not as lucky. "Blatt! She's got you already. You'll be dead before dinner. Stop interviewing her!"

She squealed in delight, the sound causing the engines to sputter. Blatt was mesmerized and began to crawl off of the wobbling vehicle. Prax set the platform's burners to full. The flying furnace instantly disintegrated a small section of the crowd, but they were able to put some distance between them and sure death.

"If you'd stop sticking your microphone anywhere you pleased, there would be less casualties," complained Prax.

Blatt shrugged but said nothing. In his mind, he was sitting on a marshmallow cloud sucking sugar milk off the teat of a lavender unicorn.

Ever the professional, Prax deflected to fight's sponsor. "We'll be back for round one right after this word from Brunhilda's Atomic-Powered Anti-Personnel Armor! Squash that misdirected uprising in style. Available in all sizes and colors."

♦♦♦

Now a familiar sound, the klaxonbot called out and Titanus responded. Giving himself heavy thumps of the fist across his chest and shoulders, his confidence surged. Once a construction worker, now deadly asskicker, the mental journey had been made. He gave a few grunts, slapped on his helmet and, gave Methil a four-fingered salute for good luck.

"Looking mean, kid!" yelled the coach. "Keep your head up."

Titanus ran out of the gate. The field was cluttered with obstacles, some he recognized as relics of his own childhood. Others, clear torture devices painted in happy Day-Glo colors that wouldn't fool a soul. Across the field, he spied a fast moving flyer. A first glance suggested a robed humanoid floating cross-legged with his arms extended. A red glow issued out from his hands.

Magic user?

Incoming fireballs confirmed. He'd have to use the playground as cover to get close enough, but as a warm up, Titanus pulled a razor-edged merry-go-round off of its pedestal and sent it soaring. It was easily dodged and the spinning wheel of death landed into a group of feral youth sporting defunct band t-shirts. Tearing through their bodies, the vociferous howl from the more athletically inclined punks sitting behind them was strangely uplifting to hear.

The magic user laughed and twiddled his fingers in a curiously familiar way. A cluster of spiked balls from the playpen in the middle of the field rose into the air and then came hurtling towards Titanus, who dove into a pile of rubber shavings and razor blades to dodge them. With his thick skin, they were far too rusty and dull to do harm.

Blatt was losing his mind. The energy of the opening round had sent him spinning. There was just simply too much color to color comment upon. By the time he figured out a lighthearted and fanciful quip about cutting, Titanus had already made his way up field, nearly within enlarging range.

"Prax, have you seen such a mismatch? Magic versus brawn? I just blew a wad in my stretch pants! I am really liking Tits. He's some kind of fighter."

The mage began a volley of ranged attacks. Fireballs and frozen meteorites at first. Titanus used the metal roof of a tool shed to deflect them as long as he could before he finally took shelter behind its brick walls. The barrage continued.

"Die, motherfucker, die!" the mage screamed.

Titanus adjusted his helm and his codpiece. There's no way I am getting beaten behind this shed.

There was a pause in the bombardment. The sound of crackling sparks, a phhhh sound, then swearing.

"Well fuckity, fuck fuck, fucking fiddlesticks. Where's that mana pot?"

Titanus took a chance and jumped out from behind the shed, if only to get a good look at the bitch.

He was surprised to see Meryzill, who was looking much better.

♦♦♦

Titanus took a tentative step toward him. "Meryzill?"

"No," said the mage, adjusting his bathrobe. "Yes. No." He paused with overdramatic flair. "Maybe."

"All right," said Titanus, taking another step forward.

"It's pronounced meh-ri-ZEEL. MER-ee-zill was my brother. How fortunate that I can avenge his death."

Titanus inched forward. The grounded mage was getting twitchy. He held out open hands and made a calming gesture to comfort him.

The crowd began to chant Titanus's name. Meryzill looked out at them. "Seriously, mana pot, please. MANA POT! Anyone?"

His plea was met with a derisive cheer. Not a merciful bunch, the youth of Peepantz. Titanus laughed under his breath. "I do not think they will help you."

Meryzill pointed to something over in the far corner. "Incoming."

Titanus looked, and with that the mage ran for his gate. Titanus sprinted in pursuit.

"You need to know that I didn't kill him," panted Titanus. "The damn fool fell on his friend's sword."

The mage ran full speed, his spindly arms pumping up and down with a comic fury. "Hey, don't judge. People can love who they want to love."

"I am NOT judging," said Titanus. Frustrated, he enlarged and lengthened an arm, grabbing Meryzill by his robe's belt. The force of his resistance caused the belt loops to break, and the belt moved up to his chest, dropping him to the ground.

Titanus stood over him. The mage held up his arms as a feeble defense. "KLAXON! When the fuck is the KLAXON!

Titanus looked up. "No klaxonbot here. Just a horde of disenfranchised youth clamoring for your death."

"Well, let it be said that my brother was no klutz," Meryzill said, neck straining to find a camera that could record his last words. "You killed him in training. You are no champion. You are the clumsy one."

"Are you done?"

The mage sighed. "Yes."

"So be it." Titanus gave him a hearty salute and jumped up and down on his skull until it was gone.

The cruel appetite of the young crowd was satiated. They responded with a deafening cheer.

"Pax Titanus!"

"Pax Titanus!"

"PAX TITANUS!"

CHAPTER THIRTEEN

His unyielding victory on the field of battle was rewarded by another sleepless night.

"Hello, sir. Mr. Titanus?"

There was a small, bluish spider monkey with glasses at the door. Titanus wiped the crust from his eyes.

"What time is it? Better be good."

"Oh sir, it is. I was requested to fetch you for a small talk with His Majesty. Your Lord, The Emperor."

Titanus stiffened. "He is here?"

"Not quite," said the monkey as he gestured to something or someone just outside the door. "Bring it in please."

Two maintenance bots wheeled in a large holomonitor.

"Very good, thank you," he said. "Now shuffle off, please."

The maintenance bots chirped. Titanus had not idea what they had communicated to the monkey, but he was fairly certain that it was contemptuous.

"Impudent bolt boxes," the monkey muttered. "Anyway, sit back and get ready for your 'Minute of Encouragement' with his grandiosity." The monkey held out a remote and turned on the monitor. The screen flickered, sputtered, and then settled on an image of a flaming, shrieking skull. Its jaws unhinged and a spleen-tickling deep moan came forth.

Panicked, the money fiddled with the remote. "Whoops, wrong channel. That's for level zero civilizations."

The image abruptly disappeared, replaced by the face of the kindly old man who had received Titanus in what seemed an age past.

"Tits, my boy, you are doing quite well!"

Titanus lowered his head slightly. "Thank you sir."

"I had always just planned on parading you around as a poster boy for teamwork. You know, one of those black, horizontal numbers with some kind of pandering slogan underneath."

"I hate those things."

"Me too, son. But they work. People eat that shit up. Anyway, you have surpassed all of my hopes. Did you hear them chanting your name today? Pure PR gold. You got a lot of pussies wet, and I know these things."

The monkey ran to the door and gestured outside once more. The maintenance bots returned, hauling a cart. On it, two comically large war hammers. Polychromatic, as they caught the light, the color of their surface changed. Their sides were adorned with carvings of fierce, screaming skulls. Where there weren't skulls, spikes had been placed.

"A gift. With your four arms, you can dual wield and still have two hands free, for slapping them or your meat. Whatever suits you."

Titanus gripped the handle of the nearest hammer. It felt like an extension of his arm, perfectly weighted and balanced.

"Go ahead Heavy Metal, test it out on those bots."

The bots attempted escape, but the monkey had locked the door. They began to chirp and whirl, begging for their lives as they zipped around the room in defensive patterns. Titanus obliged the Emperor, smashing both of them into small bits of metal and plastic. Their mechanical protests meant nothing to him.

"These are useful. Thank you."

"Oh, wait until they get a load of you," the Emperor giggled. "Your victories make me look so smart, so wise for having named you the champion. I'm afraid you'll have to win it all or I will lose face. Use these hammers well and you will avoid mine. Emperor out."

Titanus felt excitement overtake him. He couldn't wait to come up with names for his new weapons. He propped them up against the wall. "Ruin? Ruination? Ticket Puncher? The Obliviator? Crunch Daddy and the Kid? Hrmm, naming weapons is more difficult than one might first imagine." Titanus knelt down close to the hammers and whispered, "What do you think, boys? What speaks to you and your experience?"

With two shattered bots and Titanus busy hugging and kissing his new hammers, the monkey was forced to push the holomonitor out by himself. Indignant, he didn't bother to mention that there was a ninja with a ventriloquist dummy standing at the door.

◆◆◆

Titanus didn't notice the monkey leaving, but he sure as hell noticed Craxx standing in the corner of the room.

"Craxx, what are you doing here? You are supposed to be watching my family, turncoat."

"Oh buddy, don't be angry. I came bearing a message," said Craxx, his head flopping more happily than usual.

Titanus lowered his voice. "Taking this a bit lightly, don't you think? How are they? Tell me now or I'll see what one of these hammers can do to bone and flesh."

Craxx just nodded. He head flew up and down, bobbing like a balloon in the wind. Something was wrong. Titanus took a table lamp and shined it on his former friend. His skin was a paler blue than Titanus remembered. That was odd.

What was even more odd were the bolts keeping his jaw attached to his skull.

Dead.

Taking careful steps, Titanus moved to him. The ninja shifted, giving Titanus pause.

"I'm ok, really. I'm better now. Have a seat."

"I'll watch your show, but you had better have answers for me. A ninja puppeteer is no match for," Titanus grabbed his hammers. Buster and Duster!"

The ninja groaned.

"Don't like it? I will continue to work on this vexing problem. Go on."

The Craxx corpse-puppet came to life.

"First off, great job buddy. You are making a real splash. Two solid fights. All the universe is talking about it."

"I am highly motivated to succeed. And now with Masher and Basher here—"

"You're trying too hard. Just let it come organically. Anyway, from here on out, all of your fights will be high profile. This is very good."

Titanus stared at his hammers. They would get names and they would be glorious. "Go on."

"This opens the way for pure fight manipulation. You've followed our instructions to kill your opponents, and that's good," said Craxx, jaw flapping manically, "but you haven't faced any key targets yet. That is about to change."

The ninja stood and began walking Craxx's carcass about the room. It was morbidly satisfying to see him dead, but worrisome as well. Sensing tension, the ninja added a slight dance to the corpse-puppet's movements.

"Every kill from here on out will have deeply demoralizing effects on the respective home planet of your challenger. That despair can be channeled. It must be harnessed. We must be victorious. You cannot fail."

Craxx now floated directly in front of Titanus. "If you fail, the Dream Leeches will claim your son forever."

Titanus told the Craxx cadaver and his ninja handler that he understood. Immediately after, he learned that his new weapons worked well against fucking asshole ninjas.

The cleaning bot would figure out how to get the stains off the walls.

CHAPTER FOURTEEN

Prax and Blatt were working the crowd. It was a much different affair than the previous fight, as it was being held on TownSquareCenterPlaza, a shopping planet. The attendees weren't there to satisfy their desire for violence. They achieved that through regular melees over highly sought and rare consumer products. Two-for-one days, or in some circles, the Sacred Bogo, often led to deaths in the hundreds. Competition and the accumulation of material goods was a way of life and death for those that called TSCP home. Fighting for pride made no sense to them. They were there because they were told that there would be a variety of door prizes and gift bags.

It was here, on inter-dimensional holovision that Titanus would present the universe with his two new best friends, Ding and Dong.

Blatt couldn't control his laughter. Holding his microphone in front of the mighty Titanus, he had spent five solemn minutes interviewing the now-feared warrior. His meteoric rise from amateur to confident killer had been an inspiration to many, and if there was one thing Blatt knew, it was how to conduct a compelling interview. But when Titanus showed off his new hammers, their chosen names left Blatt with messy pants.

"Looks like baby made a boom-boom," he quipped as Blatt climbed back into their flying broadcast platform. Prax did not have such problems to deal with, as long as someone changed his water once a week.

"Just be happy you don't have a nose, my friend."

"So for our viewers, what was it like to sit down with The Four-Armed Terror of Veritassia?"

"Well partner, he's big. Bigger than one might expect. Those large, shredded muscles! The chest that goes on for days. His massive and perfectly toned legs—What power! And those arms, the four delicious arms that could hold you all night while he tells you that everything is going to be ok, that those terrible boyfriend who never called you back is losing out on something big, well let me just say—"

"Blatt!"

"Yeah?"

"Stay focused!"

The klaxonbot sang its song. It was time for something to die.

Blatt shifted gears quickly. "Ok folks, big one today. Titanus versus Steve." Blatt put on his reading glasses. "Steve. The Millipede of Vargas 7."

"Ohh, good fight here. Steve is a tough bastard who has been rising through the ranks of the Outer Ring circuit. We'll get right to the action, but first a word from H.G. Bloaters, the first safety glasses made for your third eye! Open portals to the darkness safely and in style. That's H.G. Bloaters!"

◆◆◆

"I am concerned," said the one-ton slug as he greedily dissolved one of his protesting underlings. "Our man seems to be doing much better than expected."

A trio of sniveling sycophantic creatures sitting at his tail nodded their heads. One was birdlike, with a crooked beak, colorful feathers, and gnarled talons. Another, a floating jellyfish with goggles. The third, a hirsute fat man in overalls.

Issuing out a small fin from its ample flesh, the slug scratched its belly.

"I am also conflicted."

The jellyfish made gurgling noises in agreement. The bird whistled. The fat man picked at his ass crack, which was a compliment in his culture.

"Roll the footage again," the slug commanded.

The holomonitor displayed Titanus's fight on Vargas 7. The first round had been a draw. The millipede moved much more quickly than Titanus, and as the arena was clogged with packages and overflowing shopping bags, there were many places for it to hide and avoid his charges.

"He doesn't do that well against speed. But he's a quick learner."

In the second round, Titanus ignored the millipede altogether and spent his time using the hammers like golf clubs, sending the obstacles flying into the crowd.

"He's clearing the field. I wonder if that was his idea or Methil's? Now the millipede has nowhere to hide. Look at him pathetically attempt to work into a crack on the side of the wall like a common silverfish."

The holomonitor offered a hundred different camera angles of the ensuing carnage.

"Then Titanus smashes the tail section with Ding. Or is it Dong? Fucking stupid names."

Titanus brought the first hammer down on the millipede. Dozens of its legs flew into the rioting crowd, which was in the middle of tearing itself apart as it fought over the gift bags that Titanus had thrown into their midst. As they destroyed themselves over sample sizes of body creams and shampoos, they chanted.

"Pax Titanus! Pax Titanus! PAX TITANUS!"

He responded by bringing down the second hammer while simultaneously increasing the size and length of his free arms so that he could grab onto Steve's cranium. The millipede fought with fury, but could not resist. Soon Titanus had his neck underfoot. The two hammers came down, one immediately followed by the other. The bug's head disintegrated instantly and a spray of green bile and blood covered the first two rows nearest the dramatic kill.

"He just coated them with poison and as they slowly die, they still chant his name. Amazing."

"You sure know how to pick them, boss," said the fat man. "This guy is going to kill his way to the top. The rebellion is a lock. The Emperor is cooked. Then we'll be in charge."

"I WILL BE in charge."

"What I said, chief."

"But as he wins, more people believe in him. This is the problem. We may not have thought this through."

The trio gulped in unison.

"Someone will have to pay. Jelly, go pull me another snack from the cages. Birdy, get ready to wipe my ass. Fat man, go check on the Dream Leeches. That kid has to stay alive for a while longer. They have a tendency to be," said the slug, "a bit too enthusiastic about their work."

◆◆◆

Titanus swung with his left, catching a jaw. The vibration of its fracture rolled through his knuckles. He quickly followed with a right, then his second left and second right in quick succession. His opponent's head was reduced to nothing but a broken egg shell encased in jellied flesh.

"I call it 'The Pulverizer' and I think it's a great trademark move for ya, Tits," said Methil as he waved off Titanus's sparring partner. The Amebite produced a sloppy, bleeding grin. Prized for their plasticity as well as regenerative abilities, they were the high-end in sparring partners and crash test dummies. Now that Titanus was a upper tier fighter, they could afford such luxuries.

"Interesting. It gives them no time to react and even if they are able to do so, they aren't going to dodge all four punches. It will be a promising move should I be disarmed."

Methil gave his massive shoulders a squeeze. "It's easy to articulate an action figure to do it too. The toy companies are going to love it."

"Action figures?"

"Oh yeah buddy. A real revenue generator. You are becoming a name, dude. Big time. Many fans. Fans need merchandise. I already took care of the contracts for you. The first Titanus toys go straight to your house. You got a son, right? He's gonna love 'em."

Titanus began doing pushups. The veins in his arms swelled as his blood pressure rose. "I do. Tinyanus."

"Miss him?"

"I do."

"We'll see if we can't swing by the house. I'm pretty sure we will have a fight near your asteroid at some point."

"Thank you."

"Time to review the holos." Methil set a small disc on the ground. It projected a perfect representation of Titanus. "Should we start with the Steve fight?"

Titanus shook his head. "The next one."

"The warrior with the laser sword?"

"The schmuck with the laser sword."

Chapter Fifteen

A schmuck with a laser sword stood near the center field sideline. Two sportscasters were interviewing him. Titanus recognized the one with the glove pants. The other, a disembodied brain, he wasn't sure. Glove pants had mocked Ding and Dong, embarrassing him enough to spend the next night brainstorming. He had even asked Rodrick's sword, Tiffany, but she couldn't think of anything better.

The schmuck with the laser sword had a mop of blonde hair and wore a pristine white tunic. He swung his weapon in an overdramatic fashion as the camera drones buzzed about. His pale humanoid skin told Titanus that he did his fighting indoors. His perfect teeth and smile suggested an innocence, a "just happy to be here" attitude.

This was the first time that he had been allowed to see his opponent before a fight. The host planet wasn't particularly memorable. It was highly civilized, very modern, and very bland. Its people were particularly boring as well, but they did seem to enjoy pomp and circumstance. Titanus had to forego his usual pre-fight routine to march in a parade, answer moronic questions from the press, and entertain fan requests for him to whip out his cock.

This circus had been going on for hours. Titanus felt bloated from eating too many appetizers, but he was bored, so eating was something to do. He did not even have Methil to keep him company. His coach had run into exotic Ventuvian Party Conjoiners, disappearing promptly as he mumbled about the cost of a 138.

The klaxon call had come as a surprise to them all. He had been in mid-chew, munching on a pastry filled with a tart, bittersweet jelly. The schmuck with the laser sword had been busy showing off some kind of minor magic, making small objects juggle and dance in the air.

Titanus ran for his hammers, scooped them up mid-stride, and ran along the edge of the arena. The crowd politely clapped and held up banners with his name written upon them. With each fight, his fan base had grown, but the signs had always been hand written and mostly featured poorly executed puns. These banners were slick and high quality. Indeed, Methil had been busy with merchandising.

He met the competition in the far corner, under the luxury suites, where the lighting was best. A quick glance upward and Titanus spied a number of celebrities, easily recognizable by their heavy body modification and the slaves that surrounded them, cooling them with fans, servicing them orally, and providing them with light snacks. In the middle, there was only one that seemed keenly focused on the fight, Grazina.

Titanus saluted her and turned to his opponent. He choked up on the handles of his hammers and swung them about in a showy and ritual fashion. The schmuck with the laser sword did the same with his.

"Why are we doing this?" said the schmuck.

Titanus motioned to the fans. "This really gets them revved up. And it gives your biceps and shoulders a nice pump."

"Oh. By the way, I'm Duke. It's an honor to fight you today."

Titanus turned his back to him and held his hammers up to the multitude of cheering spectators. "Thank you. Same. I must warn you, I do not spare my victims. I do not have the luxury to do so. My apologies."

Duke waved his laser sword about, trying to look intimidating.

"I've noticed. So be it, I guess." His voice dropped an octave. "You will put down your hammers."

"I will put down my hammers?"

"It's not a question. It's a command."

Titanus laughed. "Why are you talking in a deeper voice?"

Duke nibbled on his lip. "You will put down your hammers."

"On your head!" Titanus took a swing, but Duke held out a hand and the hammer hit ricocheted off an invisible shield.

"Normally the voice does the trick," said Duke as he performed a perfect reverse flying somersault.

Titanus took a swing with his other hammer, making contact with Duke's force field; the impact threw Duke backwards. He banked off the rounded corner of the arena and landed flat on his face.

"Who's your daddy?" said Titanus.

The audience cheered politely.

Duke jumped to his feet. He was quick and resilient, smart and powerful. Titanus knew he would have to fight intelligently. He charged Duke at full speed. The nimble laser swordsman leaped into the air and vaulted over his shoulders, his sword flittering. By the time Duke landed, three pieces of Titanus's armor had fallen to the ground. His flesh burned and small curls of smoke issued out from the scorched flesh that had moments ago been protected.

Duke pointed to him. "Drop your hammers."

The need to drop his weapons tickled the back of Titanus's skull.

"Aha. I'm getting in there a little bit." Duke pointed to a chunk of crumpled metal that sat abandoned near the fire exit. It lifted up from the ground and with a flick of his wrist, launched it directly at Titanus.

Contact!

Knocked off balance, Titanus stumbled. His ears rang and he dropped both of the hammers. His legs suddenly felt heavy.

The chunk of metal returned, knocking him over. It began to bounce up and down, first his head, then chest, and then head again. Vision blurred, Titanus looked up.

There was Grazina, screaming for him to fight, to cover himself, to do something! From the corner came the slurred sound of Methil swearing up a storm. Get off your ass!

The growing buzz of Duke's laser sword announced approaching doom. It could not end here. Titanus yelled to Grazina.

"Take it off baby, take it off!"

Without hesitation, Grazina pulled her ceremonial breastplate away. Her three ample, pendulous breasts, all three with perfect nipples, bounced happily, now free of their metallic confines. The glory of her abundant womanhood stirred Titanus in a profound way. It had been so lonely on the road.

Blood rushed to his groin, and his member responded, quickly growing rock hard. With great single-mindedness, Titanus forced his substantial erection to grow.

Enlarge!

Duke was almost upon him, a whirling dervish of laser death. Still on his back, Titanus flipped to his side to meet him, cracking the man's skull with his tumescence. Duke fell to the earth; his sword was thrown far from reach. With great determination, Titanus proceeded to use his engorged cock to batter the man mercilessly, until there was little more than a pile of unrecognizable gore.

◆◆◆

As it was the very next day, Titanus was not prepared for his next fight. All Methil had time to say before the match was, "This one is bound to be really fucking tough. Don't be stupid."

Titanus didn't have time to be stupid when he fighting three men at once. The Kevins were also unknowns that had made a name for themselves with their unique abilities. There was the Kevin who manipulated sound, then Kevin who manipulated earth, and then the Kevin who verbally abused his target and also carried a big fuck-off knife. The triplets were identical in every other way. Handsome as hell, they were clearly the media favorites that day, although the fans were behind him in full force.

A sound wave had knocked him on his ass. An eruption under the surface flung him in the air. The Kevin on his chest, riding him like a bucking bronco told him that he was ugly and his mother dressed him funny. He also punched him in the side a dozen times.

Titanus managed to pull him off and tossed him away. Sound Kevin used vibrations to soften the fall. Earth Kevin kicked up a cloud of dust to obscure his vision. Not knowing where the next attack would come from, Titanus swung the hammers wildly.

Then the bite and burn of a knife's edge across his upper thigh. The gush of warm blood down his leg.

"Nice one, Kevin."

"Thanks, Kevin. The taint is the only weak spot on this guy. Hey Tits, did your coach already cash the check? I'd ask for my money back."

"Good one, Kevin."

Another sound wave knocked Titanus over. Dirt began to pile on top of him.

"Get some distance, kid," yelled Methil from the corner.

The attacks were relentless and he could not find distance. Every time he got back on his feet, he was either toppled by another sound wave, a chunk of dirt, or was told something rude about his mother. The only thing that seemed to help was his thick hide, which prevented the knife from doing any more damage.

Methil paused the holovid. "Do you know how close you came to biting it here?"

Titanus nodded. "I felt fear for the first time. They got in my head."

"They got in your head. Your tiny little head. You Veritassians can increase the size of every body part but you head. I wonder why."

"We can increase skull density. There's that."

"I don't think you could get any more dense, kid. You're lucky that these guys are as overconfident as they are good looking." Methil pressed play.

Titanus lay prone and nearly unconscious. The arena was filled with the thunderous cries of the crowd and the chattering of the media already reporting his defeat.

"Who wants the honors? Kevin?" said Sound Kevin.

"No, Kevin. I think it should be Kevin," said Insult Kevin.

Earth Kevin clenched his fists. The ground began to rumble. "I got this, boys." With an overdramatic gesture, he threw his arms forward and the ground surged, sending a powerful undulation of dirt and dust directly at Titanus. He gritted his teeth and prepared for the impact. It sent him into the crowd, crushing the nearest section of fans. The crowd howled.

It also sent his two hammers into the air. Like trained dancers, they circled and looped poetically, before their weight sent them downward and directly onto the heads of Sound and Earth Kevin, driving them into the loosened dirt.

The excited crowd pushed Titanus back to the arena floor. With his survival instinct fully engaged, Titanus charged the triplets and unleashed a series of haymakers that removed their heads from their bodies. Three simultaneous streams of blood exploded from their necks. Titanus quickly grabbed his hammers and posed for pictures. T-shirts with the image of Titanus at blood fountain went on sale minutes later.

Methil shut off the holovid. "You got lucky. Twice. The last two fights were won because you got lucky. What happens if your opponent is luckier?"

"I understand."

"I do like that 'Pulverizer' move. That's a keeper. But you gotta use it and you gotta be smarter, kid. You got two more fights. You win those, you'll go to the finals."

And with the finals, my son.

"Now the good news here is that although we can't predict who you will fight, the field is getting smaller and I have a few good guesses. I'm going to show you some tape of this Kakuian fighter, Massst Handergassst. This fucker is tearing it up in another bracket. We gotta hope somebody takes him out. I can't think of a fighting style that would be a worse matchup for you."

CHAPTER SIXTEEN

Prax and Blatt were having a hard time working the crowd. Alfreedians were known for their aloofness. A highly intelligent and obnoxiously arrogant people, Alfreedians enjoyed extremely long lives and the crankiness that comes from hundreds of years of suffering life's unending parade of bullshit. They were so pissy about everything that they rarely left their homes, often too busy protecting their carefully landscaped lawns and praying for a respectable bowel movement. Tonight, the vast majority of the attendees were virtual, either solid form holograms or cybernetic avatars. There were maybe a dozen living and breathing Alfreedians in the whole place. Most likely they were court mandated to attend.

Blatt picked up his radio. "Prax, I'm not getting any good pre-game stuff here. Every time I ask a question, they show me their hand."

"Get coverage. We'll talk over it. They dress nicely, and we can play that up. They love it when their fashions are praised, even though they would never admit it. Compliment them on their nice skin and pointy ears, too. They are stupidly vain."

Titanus performed his warm-ups. Methil smoked his cigar. It had all become routine.

"Not hearing the crowd, Methil. You know that's my fuel."

"Sure Tits, every fighter needs to hear the call of his bloodthirsty fans. Ain't that kind of planet. These bastards are shoe gazers. Hyper emo and hip. Fuck 'em. Do what you do. There's a bigger audience watching than just the one on this stick-up-the-ass planet. The whole universe is watching you now." Methil began to rub him down with heating gel. "Stay limber. Shit gets real fucking tough now. No doubt they got a beast lined up for you. You good?"

Titanus slammed his hammers together. "Pumped."

"Stay smart. Don't get yourself in the corner. Use your abilities. If he's big, you get big. You don't always remember to do that."

The klaxonbot sounded its horn and Titanus ran through the gate. The arena was nearly silent. Only a few of the Alfreedians even bothered a golf clap.

Huh, thought Titanus, trying to rev them up with some bicep curls and chest pumping.

Nothing.

Even the veteran broadcasters were surprised by the blasé vibe of the arena.

Blatt leaned into his microphone. "Tough room, Prax! Unbelievable that nobody cares. This is Titanus, after all."

"They don't know what they are about to see, Blatt," said Prax. "Titanus pulled a Brain Squealer as an opponent. In fact, we don't know what we are going to see either. This is going to be very interesting. The fact that arbitrary rules have determined that there is no time limit for this match makes is even more so. Let's watch."

After attempting to prime the audience, Titanus turned to face his latest challenge. There was nothing to be seen. He called out. "Uh, hello?"

No reaction from the crowd. An invisible challenger?

Titanus began swinging his hammers in wide circles, hoping that he might catch his opponent mid-charge.

Nothing. He walked around the arena, searching behind every half-wall, barricade, and obstacle. His arms had grown tired. He looked to Methil, who was flying about, violently waving his arms back at him. His coach was clearly yelling, but he couldn't hear a thing.

Then, a small voice from underfoot.

"Excuse me, sir," said a small, furry creature. It had the largest, roundest eyes he had ever seen. It had tiny hands and was painfully cute. "Have you seen my parents?"

Titanus pushed up his helm with one of his hammers in order to see the small child.

"Hi kid. Are you lost?"

It started crying, its small body heaving rapidly. "I don't know where I am! Please help me."

Titanus took a look around. The Alfreedians, so uncaring, stood and sat in place, barely moving. The outer edge of the arena took on a blurry, sepia-tone hue. A brilliant shaft of sun broke through the clouds and cast a golden light down upon them.

That is a beautiful sun, thought Titanus. "Let's get you out of here. I think the fight has been postponed or something."

The creature stopped crying and perked up. "That'd be great, mister."

They began to walk. The exit gate seemed so very far away.

"Of course. I have a son of my own. I would hope that if he was lost, someone might help him as well."

"I know. I met him."

"You met my son?"

Titanus's legs tired. How long had they been walking? The gate seemed no closer.

"I talk to him all the time."

The creature stopped and turned. It looked at him with its ridiculously adorable eyes.

"He fucking hates you."

Titanus felt his knees buckle.

"He says you allowed him to be kidnapped. That you will let him die. That you can't protect him," It giggled.

Titanus felt so heavy. "That's not true. He knows how much I love him. How much I would do for him. He's the reason why I'm here." The ground pulled him down to meet it.

From the broadcast dais, the view was very different.

"I don't believe what I am seeing!" yelled Blatt. "Titanus walked right up to the Brain Squealer and—"

Prax interrupted. "Just let it wrap its tendrils around him. See the base of his neck? It's drilling in. It won't be long before it pierces his brain."

"What a way to go, Prax. I think I'd prefer to bang some five-credit hookers, contract Flesh Rot, and watch my body dissolve as I screamed in agony instead of dying in the grips of that beast. At least I'd get some cards and flowers from my friends and loved ones. Contracting a fatal disease can make a man feel special."

"I don't think there are many that would disagree with that, Blatt."

Titanus was having difficulty breathing. The cuddly creature was now sitting on his chest.

"Poor daddy. He's going to die now. And so will his son." Its eyes expanded, a sea of whiteness that contrasted the minuteness of its pupils. It leaned in close. Its breath smelled of sugar-dusted berries and cotton candy.

But in its glee, it had leaned in too close and in the milky white of its eyes; Titanus could see a flicker of a beast hiding within. Its mouth was filled with jagged hooks that pulled thick strings of saliva between them as its maw widened.

With tears in his eyes, Titanus knew he could do only one thing. With what little energy he had remaining, he slapped all four of his hands together and smashed the small, furry boy; like a grenade, its body popped, sending fur shrapnel and bloody entrails in every direction.

Titanus now sat in pile of lifeless tendrils and intestines. Bile dripped off his nose and down his cheeks. The monstrosity's spherical, cartoon eyes bounced twice before rolling to a stop at his feet. He sighed, Methil screamed victory, and the couldn't-care-less attitude of the crowd gave way to a thousand nods of Alfreedians that were duly impressed.

CHAPTER SEVENTEEN

Methil looked proud as hell. He stood next to a large crate.

"I don't like the look on your face. What do you have there?" asked Titanus.

"I've been saving it for this moment, kid. This is the last fight in this bracket. You win this, it will be a title fight for sure." Buzzing happily, he opened up the box. Inside, gleaming, ornate armor that featured images of his various kills. The chest piece had a highly detailed skull with curved horns etched onto its surface.

"You gotta look the part. You gotta look like a champion."

Titanus ran his hand over the metal. It gave his fingers a tingle.

"But I already have that armor you gave me."

"This isn't from me. It's from the Emperor."

"It's very well made. Clearly from the hands of a expert blacksmith."

"To yours. It's fully articulated for your specific ranges of movement. It has a light anti-gravity charge so you will never feel its weight."

Titanus put on the armor and stood in front of the mirror. He looked even better than he thought he would.

"Now that's the look of a champion!" Methil grinned. "You do me proud. And you've helped me. Going through this tournament as your coach, hell, I thought I knew it all. But I didn't. Every fight you pull something out of your ass. To be honest, I didn't even know if you would make it out of that first one with the Muggottth."

"Neither did I."

"And look at you now. One fight away from the big banana. One kill away from a shot at the title."

"Just one more."

"One more kill. That's an absolute requirement for the next round. You have to kill your opponent."

Titanus looked at himself in the mirror. He held both hammers up and posed.

"I will kill my opponent without hesitation. The title must be mine."

◆◆◆

Viet 12 was a nasty place. The entire planet was a enormous dank swamp. With each step, Titanus sank deeper into the mud and water, nearly to his knees. Unease set in when he saw his opponent fly out of their gate and make a quick ascent into the sun.

Methil yelled motherfucker this and that. Prax and Blatt got wet over the possibilities. The spectators, watching from large anti-grav platforms, their "Pax Titanus" banners displayed proudly, gasped in unison. Their favorite gladiator would be at a serious disadvantage.

Titanus tried to block out the sun's glare with one of his free hands. The flyer had chosen the perfect spot to linger. Its form was backlit, making its features impossible to discern. The glowing light behind it only added to Titanus's creeping worry.

Methil yelled from the sidelines. "I told you it would be tough, kid! Take out the wings first!"

Titanus dropped into a fighting stance that would give him the most stability he could manage standing in a few feet of mud. The flyer tightened its wings against its body as it dipped down into an plummeting dive. Titanus readied his hammers. As the flyer zoomed downward, he heard a familiar war cry.

Gleedrial.

She stopped her attack short and fluttered her wings gently.

"Hey big stuff," she said.

Titanus lowered his hammers. "How can this be?"

Gleedrial sprouted a sheepish grin. "I'm a stone cold killer, Tits. I told you I was a ringer. And now here I am."

"This will not do. I have no desire to kill you. You were a good friend to me when I arrived."

"I have something to tell you, but take a look around. The fans, we are confusing the fuck out of them." Gleedrial motioned to the crowd, Prax and Blatt, and finally to Methil. No one seemed to be able to make sense of the lack of murder on the field.

"Pretend we are sparring, but make it look convincing." She flew back up into the air, performing theatrical moves with her spear. Titanus

82

responded by making grunts and striking poses with his hammers. The cameradrones squealed with happiness at the marketability of the footage they were capturing. What a highlight reel it would be.

"It would appear that the two know each other," said Blatt. "This has never happened before. Can you imagine, Prax? Can you imagine if we had to fight each other?"

"Every day," said Prax.

Gleedrial was relentless with Titanus, zipping to and fro, sneaking in a strike of her spear wherever she could, but mostly aiming directly for his armor to limit the possible damage. Titanus swung hammer, then hammer, then fist, then fist; he couldn't connect a single blow. There were a few that came close, but when they did, he would inexplicably lose his balance and only caught air. Had this been a true fight, he would have not had a chance. She would have killed him instantly.

"I like the new armor," she said flying by. "You look like quite a stud. I'm coming in for a buzz-by. I want you to grab me by the throat. Don't squeeze though. I don't want anything to happen to you."

"Come at me," Titanus said, doing exactly as she said. He pulled her out of the air with little effort. The crowd responded with delight. She was now in his grasp. It gave him a perplexing sense of pleasure to have her so close.

"Ok, now I can pretend I am pleading for my life while I give you the what's what."

"Go on. I will be careful."

"I told you I'm a ringer. Can't be killed by normal means. Charmed." Her skin gave off an otherworldly glow, the same he had seen back in training. "I'm the Emperor's girl. I clean out the riffraff. Kinda what you are doing for the rebels."

"I do not—fuck, I cannot lie. Yes. But I have a noble purpose. Tinyanus."

Gleedrial smiled. "I know all about it. Beautiful kid. But shit's gone south, Tits. Emperor thinks you are too popular now. He's getting jealous. Wants the 'Citizen's Champion' to go out a martyr. Kidnappers want you to die in the championship, thinking the Emperor will lose face. It's a no-win scenario. The only sure thing that will happen is that you will die and your son will most likely live. Got the inside big picture on that."

She began to squirm. "Let me fight you a little," she said. Titanus repositioned and Gleedrial feigned a struggle. Gritting her teeth she said, "You are going to die, but not now, not by me. You get me?"

"Are you telling me to kill you? This match is ruled to end in death."

"Rebels want me dead because of my service to the Emperor. But, there's that whole immortal thing I've got. I don't know what they are expecting you to do that they can't."

Titanus began to loosen his grip on her neck. "I do not wish to kill you."

From her eyes, a golden light flowed outward. It circled his arms and began to flow upward to his torso. "But you must. This is my love for you, Titanus. Not a carnal love, but the love of one true being for another. Embrace it. Remember it. Remember me."

Titanus paused and allowed her energy to penetrate his tough skin. She knew his truth.

"The klaxon will sound in a moment. When you go to your corner, grab Rodrick's sword Tiffany. You will be able to kill me with it. And when this is over, see a doctor. Immediately. Something's not right with you."

Titanus opened his hand and she hurtled toward her gate as the klaxonbot marked the end of the round.

◆◆◆

"Give me the sword," Titanus barked.

Methil grabbed the duffle bag. "The one that never shuts up? Seriously?"

"Do it. I need a magical weapon to kill her."

Methil used a pair of tongs to fish the sword out of the bag.

"Well, hello!" said Tiffany. "Finally!"

Methil brought the sword to him. Titanus reached out to grab it.

"Now hold on, baby. Once you grab me, you can never let go. We'll be soul mates! That work for you?"

Methil winced. "You'll always be at hand? Pun intended, sweetheart."

Titanus clenched the sword. He felt the muscles in his forearm spasm and lock. He was now hers and she was now his. "I do what I must. That is what I do. We will figure this out later."

"Magic," she whispered.

The second round began.

◆◆◆

Gleedrial fought fiercely and with tenacious spirit. Determined to put on a good show, she continued to avoid mortally wounding Titanus, generously giving him some opportunities to get his licks in. Tiffany bleated with joy every time her edge found purchase. Still, all were surprised when Gleedrial left her sternum unprotected and Titanus drove the sword through her.

Silent, the crowd held their mouths open in abatement.

Titanus pushed in close and met her eye to eye. "Thank you," he said."

Her golden light slowly faded from her gaze. Gleedrial put a reassuring hand on his shoulder and whispered, "It's ok. I needed a break. You know what to do next."

She pushed herself further up on the blade and expired. All light left her form.

Tiffany exploded with joy. "We did it! We killed her! Yum, yum, her blood tastes like candy! So very sweet!"

"Yes, Tiffany. We killed her. Now shut up," he sniffed.

There was no time to process what had just occurred. Cameradrones and the ever-present Prax and Blatt quickly surrounded Titanus. His face disappeared in a sea of microphones. Most of their questions were banal, but one thing was clear. He was going to the final round.

The crowd cheered. "Pax Titanus! Pax Titanus! PAX TITANUS!"

Balloons dropped. Confetti was tossed. Gleedrial's body was removed honorably to the tune of bagpipes.

Blatt wheeled in a holomonitor. "Special surprise for the big winner! I've got your wife here for you."

There she was. Hiediiee, waving her tentacles happily. For any casual viewer, what they saw was a happy wife excitedly celebrating her husband's brutal victory. But Titanus saw something else. A pool of hot pink secretion underneath her flailing appendages.

She was frightened. He put his hand to the monitor but it was quickly whisked away. Methil joined him and started to field the remaining questions. Titanus's head felt light. His lower left leg burned. It was covered in insect bites. Viet 12 sucked balls.

He fell over from exhaustion.

CHAPTER EIGHTEEN

The Doctorborbot frowned. It took an incredibly bad diagnosis to cause an artificial form to do so. They usually didn't give a shit.

"It appears that a Reversal Worm has infected you. The bane of Viet 12. The cool kids call them 'Ragers.' This insidious beast adapts to your physiology and uses it against you. It can kill very quickly. You have to stop fighting immediately," it said as it did something official-looking with its clipboard.

Titanus did his best to balance himself on the edge of the examination table but his immensity made it an exercise in comic futility. The room was also too small as it was made for more reasonably sized beings. The Doctorborbot didn't acknowledge the fact that nearly every corner of the room was jammed with some part of Titanus's physique. The poor warrior was a goddamn pretzel.

"My next fight it the title fight. I can't quit," said Titanus.

"The more you use your abilities, the sooner you will die. You need your power to fight, no?"

Titanus nodded. "It's all I have. That, the fact that I bench press small asteroids, two war hammers, and this enchanted blade that is now permanently attached to my hand."

Tiffany whistled. "Hello, Doctorborbot!"

"Right." The Doctorborbot also nodded, recognizing Titanus's nod and wishing to respond ironically. "Well maybe stick with those and avoid enlarging. Every time you increase your size, the worm works its way deeper into your DNA. Eventually you will explode at the atomic level, making you a worm bomb that will infect anyone in your proximity."

Titanus nodded again, which made the Doctorborbot somewhat uncomfortable as at this point they both looked a bit ridiculous. "How long do I have?"

"If you say, concentrated your ability and used it only at certain times or for certain body parts, you could extend your fighting life to say, about ten minutes. Well, ok, take care and all that—"

Titanus put three of his mighty palms on the Doctorborbot's chest. "Ten minutes? I need to win the championship. There can be no hindrance. Surely there is something I can do."

"There is something, but as you are a Veritassian, you won't like it."

The gladiator pulled him closer. "Tell me."

"Apologize."

"I'm sorry," Titanus said as he released his grip. "I'm just frustrated."

The Doctorborbot smoothed his lab coat. "Not to me, but thank you. You must apologize to every one you have ever hurt. That puts the worm into a hibernation of sort. It feeds off of aggressive energy. How much time do you have before this fight?"

Titanus was not pleased. "Two weeks. They need time to properly cross-promote the fight through every available communication channel. But it matters little. I do not apologize to anyone. They knew the risks."

"This is true, and as a Veritassian, you operate with singular motivation. Pride, love, hate. An extensive mea culpa is far too layered. Too complex. I understand."

"As do I. I much as it violates my personal beliefs I will follow your advice and," he stumble over the words, "a-po-lo-gize. I must win the championship. I just need to be good for one more fight. That's all I need."

"Then you should be able to pull it off. After you win, it's going to be a short celebration. No amount of apologies will stop the worm forever. Make it count."

"Thanks, Doctorborbot."

"You can just call me Torborbot. No need for formalities. Pay at the counter, please."

◆◆◆

Methil scratched his head. "Apologize? For what? Smells like bullshit to me. Never heard of these Reversal Worms."

"Apparently every one I have hurt." Titanus started to pack a bag.

"You ain't going anywhere, kid. We have a fight to train for, and it's that Massst guy. He's full of surprises. We need to strategize."

Titanus stuffed two pairs of gloves into the bag. The sword kept getting in the way, threatening to shred his luggage as he packed. "If I don't, I'm going to die, Methil."

"Kid, you're definitely going to die if you don't prepare. Besides, who's left to apologize to? You killed all of them. With fucking style, I might add."

It was impossible not to smile. He had been kicking serious ass. "I've investigated. Duke is on life support on General Receiving Station 12. I'm going."

Methil poured a shot of something into his coffee. "Shitballs. You might as well stop home and visit your wife too. I did promise you that. Make the most of the time you're losing here, and between Massst and these goddamn worms, you might as well get your final nut out."

The sword twinkled. "Wait until she meets me. The seductive other woman."

Methil put a finger to his mandible as he began to slide a scabbard over Tiffany.

"Not fair. I have every right to—"

"How is it that you haven't done that sooner?" asked Titanus.

"Never thought to do it. Didn't even know if it would work."

Titanus hugged Methil so hard that he almost shattered his coach's thorax.

◆◆◆

Duke had seen better days. Currently he was a disorganized pile of bone matter, squashed tissue, and translucent goop.

"Step away from the sneeze guard, sir," said the orderlybot as it wiped down the thick plastic shield that protected Duke's innards. "Three foot minimum. Hands off the glass."

Titanus obediently took a step back, leaving a thin layer of his sweat behind. He was not feeling well. Deep down, swimming in his essence, the Ragers were busy.

"What exactly is going on here?"

"He's being recombined, obviously," said the orderlybot. "Getting his parts all sorted out."

"Can he hear me?"

The orderlybot scanned the pile of entrails. "I don't see a fucking ear. Do you see a fucking ear?"

"IT WAS A REASONABLE QUESTION!"

The robot cocked its head, and then pushed a few buttons on its chest. They happily chirped back at it. "I'm sorry, sir. I was set to 'sassy.' I have readjusted my response center to 'empathically concerned.' How may I help you?"

"I just wanted to know if he could hear me?"

"Ah," said the orderlybot as it began to dust off the machines that were keeping Duke's fleshy bits alive. "I want you to know that I hear you and respect you. Most likely he cannot, as he is currently an unfortunate pile of gook and glop. Take your best shot. I am sure that the gesture is appreciated."

Titanus waited until the robot sped off. His stomach felt like a fist was pulling it into a knot. "Duke, I don't know if you are there, but I have something to tell you."

The pile of Duke did not register a response. It might have slightly shifted. Titanus couldn't be certain. It could have just been the lighting. He looked over at the monitor, but there was no change in the measured signal. Just a straight line that travelled across the screen, taking a moment to spike at seemingly random times.

"You fought well. You fought with honor. I fought better," Titanus could feel a stammer coming on. "I know you knew the risks." Sweat poured down his forehead. His throat became dry. Down his back, a ripple of nervous flesh made its way down to the crack of his ass.

"But I just."

Find the words! Find them or die!

"I want to say."

Fuck, say it.

"I'm sorry."

The monitor chirped rapidly. Duke had heard him. Titanus felt some of the tension melt away from his body. The deep down pain subsided. The sweating stopped. The monitor's chirping turned into a siren. Titanus slapped the sneeze guard. "Thank you, Duke. I knew you would respect the warrior code. That's a real load off. See you later."

Titanus turned and left the room knowing that he had just bought some time. Doctorborbots pushed past him. Clearly they were in a hurry.

"Best of luck, guys. Thanks again," said Titanus.

"CODE MUTHERFUCKING BLUE!" announced the Doctorborbots.

CHAPTER NINETEEN

Home. Titanus was home.

He stood in the doorway to his son's bedroom. Surrounded by his stuffed plushies, Tinyanus was in the Deep Sleep. Large plasma creatures swirled around his peaceful rest.

"Any change? At all?"

Titanus's wife wrapped her tentacles around him. She was oozing yellow slime. Slowly, he began to absorb her thoughts. Squeezing her back, he said, "This will end soon. Once I kill Massst Handergassst in the finals, the Dream Leeches will release our son. We will get him back. This I swear."

Blue bile began to seep from several of her pseudopods. She was anxious. Titanus gave her a consoling pat to her nerve cluster.

"Fear not for me, my wife. As is our way, my fight is more important than my life. Should I die in the arena, do not weep. I have crushed skulls, smashed rib cages, and torn out living hearts. None will stop me. None have stopped me. I even did that whole apologizing business."

He sensed her confusion. He picked her up and moved her to one of her plastic covered seating platforms.

"I am not well. In my last fight, Reversal Worms infected me. They are rewriting my DNA as we speak."

Her limbs became tense. She began to secrete more blue bile, but it quickly turned pink.

"Do not be frightened, my love. I have taken steps to momentarily silence the worms. They require a kindness to inhibit their attack, but they are inevitable. Remember my fight against Duke? I apologized to him while he was on life support. I looked like a damn fool apologizing to a pile of squashed flesh and bone, but I did it. I did it for little Tinyanus and you. My devotion, this may not come naturally to you, but I want you to celebrate my truth. It is the way of my people."

Titanus felt a smaller appendage enter his ear canal. With it, more ooze. Waves of worries thought flowed through him.

"The rebels are vile beasts, but they are honorable extortionists. I have met the Emperor. He is mentally unbalanced and his tyranny is well known. The rebels only stole Tinyanus's consciousness because they knew I had the best chance to destroy some of their enemies. People that were in the way. It's not personal. I brought this upon us by saving Craxx and those people from an atomic apocalypse, but there is not a universe where I would not have done so. Such is my path."

He gave her a tight squeeze, taking care to keep Tiffany behind his back. The scabbard had done well to silence her. "Don't get all knotted up. Last time it took half a year to get you undone."

Hiediiee would have laughed, but it took too long to work up the enzymes.

◆◆◆

As Titanus lied down on the bed, welcoming its comforting embrace. For a sliver of a second, the memory of his simple life once lived came rushing back, overtaking him with emotions. Work, love, fear, hate, and sadness came in unstoppable waves. His body shuttered from the fierce blitz of feelings.

Then another recognizable feeling came to the forefront; he was horny as hell. Of course, having a wife gushing emotion juice all over him made it impossible to not feel something but it would have made things easier if it hadn't been everything at once.

Hiediiee sat square on his chest, leaking fluid in order to set the mood. She began to unfurl her tentacles, becoming a fan of glazed, slippery flesh. Slowly, all the various colors of her secretions turned to a uniform and vibrant green. Titanus smiled as he watched her outer labia pull back. Now he was truly home. Her first clitoris began to swell and he rewarded it by rubbing it gently, first forward and back, then left to right. He topped it off with a swirling motion.

Gentle vibrations came from deep within her nerve center, thanking him for his touch.

"I've missed you," he said.

Her limbs were now fully fanned. Titanus took another free hand and ran it along one of her major tentacles. He lingered long enough to allow her intimate seepage to be fully absorbed by his skin. Never had he felt such carnal longing from Hiediiee, She hadn't been this ready to go since their third date, when Titanus had crippled one of her former suitors to show his dominance.

As her ferocious sexual need spoke to him at a cellular level, she unfurled her second set of labia, then the third. Two more glorious clits made their presence known, and Titanus used his two remaining free hands to rub them as well. He kept his now permanent sword hand low to the floor, but did not notice the scabbard sliding off. As Hiediiee began to fully pulsate she showered him with her juices and he knew she was ready. Pushing past her remaining two sets of fleshy lips, Titanus's throbbing member thrust into her center mass. For the next four hours, he pushed with all that he had to give.

In one night, the totality of their love was demonstrated by a series of rolling, multi-staged mutual orgasms that left both of them sweaty and slime covered. One could not hope for a better goodbye love fuck. They collapsed in pure joy for their deep and binding connection.

From the floor came a female voice.

"Wow, you are such a stud, Tits. That was mind-blowing," said Tiffany.

CHAPTER TWENTY

Being that it was the title fight, a concerned Titanus worked a sparring bot over with gusto, trying to teach himself how to pull of his "Pulverizer" move off with three arms instead of four. With Tiffany permanently mounted to his lower right arm, it required some adjustments. The upshot was that she could be used for a spectacular killing blow, and Titanus found that dangerously thrilling. He had destroyed four sparring bots in less than an hour. The massive, cutting-edge gym was happy to oblige. It could manufacture new sparring bots in-house. He was free to wreck as much shit as possible.

"That's the stuff, kid. Nice twist on your killing blow," offered Methil as he poured a shot of whiskey into his coffee. "Fuck it up."

Titanus wiped the sweat off his forehead and grunted his appreciation. His muscles swelled with anticipation for the upcoming fight, but the subcutaneous squirming of the Ragers reminded him that the clock was ticking.

"Don't worry about it, Tits," said Methil as he gave Titanus a light shoulder rubdown. "It's a tough break, but I still got a good feeling about this. Hell, win tomorrow and there will be so much money flying around that I'm sure we can hook up a cure for you." Methil buzzed over to his worktable and shuffled through some papers. "Says here to expect the Emperor. Surely he has the juice to take care of this. You are his champion. How would it look if you died out of combat?"

"Out of combat?"

"Yeah, like on the shitter clutching your chest with Ragers coming out of your asshole. Now pay attention. Massst is a tough opponent. There's a reason why he's made it to the finals. You had a lotta luck helping along. Not Massst —he's never needed it. He's won every fight decisively."

Methil pushed a chalkboard up to the front of the training room. "I got a few things to go over." He proceeded to draw an incredibly complex flowchart. There was a lot of math.

"What does this have to do with crushing his skull?" asked Titanus.

"Yeah, let's just stab the little bitch," added Tiffany.

Methil chomped down on his cigar. "Tiff, I like your enthusiasm. We'll need it. But you're magic and this is science, so just pay attention, ok?"

"Go on, why am I looking at a math problem?"

"Massst Handergassst is a Kakuian. You know about those guys?"

"That they are a standard bipedal humanoid species. Rather pale skin. They speak with an atrocious lisp. They dress oddly. Their clothing features a lot of ruffles and other extraneous bits of fancy."

"Correct on all accounts, but there's a critical trait they possess that has the potential to fuck your world up."

Methil made a general gesture at the board. "They live out of phase. Out of time. They live in a dimension that rubs up against ours," Methil said, pantomiming an ass rubbing up against his stinger. "Their dimension is about one second ahead of ours, but shares our space."

Titanus rubbed his temples. "I am having difficulty with this concept."

"So is the Interdimensional Naturalization Service." Methil flew over to one corner of the room. "Ok, I'm here, right? You see me right here? How far do you think I can fly in one second?"

Titanus pointed to the floor in front of the chalkboard.

"Not a bad guess, but no," said Methil as he buzz-bombed Titanus's now aching head. "I'm here in one second, and I'm slashing your neck. Wherever you see Massst, he's actually one second closer and you won't know until it's too late. You will have to anticipate. And Tiffany, you have to help."

"Roger dodger," said the sword.

"Now get some rest. By this time tomorrow, you'll either be dead or the greatest warrior in the universe. I like your odds, so have confidence."

Titanus didn't doubt that he could win, but it did little to help him sleep.

◆◆◆

It had been decided that the casino planet Kamari would host the final fight. Its people were known for gambling on anything that could produce numerical odds and the local bookies had been busy generating bets on everything from the winner of the contest to the chance that Kamari would suddenly fall into its own sun.

Also, they had the best hookers, and if there was one thing the universe loved, it was hookers. If there was a second thing, it was cocks. Much love for the cock, which is why fans in all manners of undress were currently waving many banners proclaiming "Pax Titanus."

The crowd was ready, a volcano waiting to explode in a frenzy of bloodlust and high fives. From their floating platforms, they screamed down below at Prax and Blatt as they performed their pre-fight banter. This championship match was promised to be the most exciting in the five hundred year history of the tournament and the lead-up promotions had included the usual media parades, psionic dream/desire intrusions, and holo talk shows, setting it up to be the ultimate meeting of indomitable strength versus supreme cunning.

"I think that Titanus may have finally met an opponent that matches his skill as a gladiator," said Prax.

"I agree, but let's see what this guy has to say," said Blatt as he shoved his microphone in the face of a large walrus-type thing. Its many rolls of fat made it difficult to know exactly where its face was, but Blatt was a professional.

"That's my ass," the walrus said.

Blatt repositioned the microphone. The crowd was so completely absorbed in pre-fight hype that he hoped no one would notice the faux pas. He decided not to acknowledge his mistake; after all, he was a true journalist. "You were saying?"

The walrus cleared its throat. "Yes. It's been quite a ride for the Pax Titanus train. Up until now, he's faced standard foes and although a few were challenging, I don't think anyone ever had a doubt that he would make it to the finals."

Prax interrupted. "Not true. Most thought he'd make it to the quasi-semi-regional-quarters. Maybe."

The walrus pointed a flipper at Prax. "They doubted his strength. His pure power. And the fact that he can enlarge his form or any part of his anatomy ten times its normal mass. I counter with the fact that this makes him formidably strong and a bit unpredictable. And let's not forget the hammers. And that smoking hot sword."

"But that doesn't work with an opponent that exists one second in the future," Blatt said in a momentary lapse of incompetence.

95

"True, he's never faced an opponent on a Kakuian Clock. I believe he will figure it out. I believe he will prevail."

Blatt gave Prax's brain chamber a nudge with his elbow. "Total bandwagon, huh?"

Before the walrus could respond, the referee's psionic whistle blew three times, triggering fifteen deaths by seizures and causing two elderly humanoids to crap their adult diapers. The rambunctious spectators silenced themselves to listen to the Emperor address the crowd. It wasn't so much that they wanted to hear what he had to say, it was the fear of being executed for insolence that kept them in line.

◆◆◆

The Emperor, as expected, had his own special flying platform. Unlike the others, which hovered by anti-grav, his was powered by hundreds of fetal slaves, all equipped with cybernetic hoverwings. The strain of keeping the incalculably heavy structure in the air killed dozens every minute, but they were immediately replaced. A staff of castrated janitors quickly swept the small corpses from the arena floor.

He was dressed in his most formal, high-court attire; he had a rooster chest of pride as he stood in his plasma robe, a swirling spectrum of color that with prolonged staring caused late-onset mental illnesses. A brief glance only caused projectile vomiting. His crown, made entirely of farm-raised, single-celled psionic organisms, glowed with the collective energy of their thought-stealing power. His scepter was a simple toilet plunger encased in a skin of gold and jewels.

He had come to rock out with his cock out.

"My fair citizens," he boomed, "it has finally come to this. The greatest fight of all time! Your 'Citizen's Champion' against the foul and conniving Kakuian, Massst Handergassst, who although a complete piece of shit, has fought his way here! Out of respect, I will attempt a modicum of objectivity." He snickered. "Who am I kidding? You all know who should win! Pax Titanus!"

The crowd obediently, yet enthusiastically, chanted.

"Pax Titanus!"

"Pax Titanus!"

"PAX TITANUS!"

"Yes, my happy little puppies. Pax Titanus! Of course, there is a chance he could lose, but them's the breaks. Am I right?"

The crowd chuckled nervously. The Emperor surveyed their obvious disingenuous, sycophantic reply.

"Relax, it's not like I'd execute anyone before the match."

Up in Row 11,235, Seat AAA11113333z, a small, round man let out a sigh. "Thank god," he said, "Cause Titanus doesn't have a fucking chance."

The Emperor gestured for his guards to arrest him.

"I said before the match! We will kill you immediately afterwards! Ha! Now let's get this party started!"

Blatt grabbed his microphone. "And that's all the motivation we need. We'll be right back with the title fight after this message from Harry's Hunting Clones. Tired of killing rare, exotic creatures? Looking for a new challenge? How about hunting and killing yourself?"

CHAPTER TWENTY-ONE

Titanus came out roaring murder. Previous arenas had filled the playing surface with obstacles and traps but here there was nowhere to hide. The grandiosity of the build-up to the fight was starkly contrasted by the plain dirt surface of the arena. It was bleak and apocalyptic.

"Let's fuck this guy up!" yelled Tiffany.

On the other side, Massst made his appearance. His halting movements made him difficult to track. He appeared standing in one place, then another, then another. It was clear that he was perfectly in tune with his abilities and knew exactly how to use them in a manner that was both disorienting and disturbing. A sick grin seemed permanently slapped on his otherwise featureless, smooth face and his fancy, formal attire felt like a taunt. The ruffles of his shirt collar and cuffs were a straight up fucking mockery of the brutal nature of the contest.

The Ragers swam dangerously near the surface of his already sweaty skin; the pain starting early for Titanus, but he did not hesitate. There was too much at stake. He moved to close the distance between them quickly.

Massst was upon him sooner than expected.

Tap, tap. The Kakuian rapped his fingers on Titanus's helmet, but when Titanus tried to swat him in return, he was no longer there. Then a tickle to the side and a slap on the butt. Again, Titanus tried to give him a wallop, but each time, he found nothing but air.

"He's testing your reflexes, boss," suggested Tiffany. "Do something unexpected."

The sound of whooshing air flew past his ears. "Yesssssssss. Something unexpected."

Titanus grunted and performed a reverse of his "Pulverizer" move, punching outwards with all of his limbs simultaneously. His fists were rewarded by making solid contact, striking Massst with considerable force. He watched as Massst bounced backwards, skipping like a stone, on his ass here then there, then finally landing.

He lay in the dirt moaning and no longer moved about in a flickering manner.

Blatt, along with everyone watching, went ballistic. "HOLY FUCKSTICKS! Did you see that?"

"I heard it. Crunch city, population one," said Prax.

The crowd screamed "Pax Titanus!" and everyone was very pleased but him. He could feel the Ragers burrowing deeper into the meat of his muscles.

There was little time left.

◆◆◆

Massst moaned. Titanus decided to close and end the fight quickly.

Tiffany squealed and said, "Let me get a taste of that shit." Titanus grunted his approval and broke into a lumbering trot toward his fallen foe.

"Solid hit, my friend. I misjudged," wheezed Massst. "That will not happen again."

Titanus stopped short, pulled his weight down and leapt, hoping to crush his enemy. His feet found nothing but dirt. Behind him, cobra bites of a sharp blade struck in rapid succession and blood spurted out from dozens of newborn wounds.

Then another whisk of air in his ears. "How does thhhhhat feel, mothhhhherfuckkkkkker?"

Titanus responded by punching randomly while Tiffany swept in large, probing circles. He could see Massst jumping about, close then far. He clenched his blade and grinned manically. Blood coated it from tip to hilt. The Kakuian was a blur, racing left then right. A dozen more wounds opened up on Titanus's thick arms.

Massst jeered and gibed as he danced, making derisive quips along the way. Each word uttered came from different location. An insult that began with a finger in Titanus's chest ended behind him or to his side; each punctuated with another stab of Massst's substantial shank.

Massst's words bounced about.

"The Citizens'... champion... will... be... the Citizen's... corpse... hahaha.... fuck... er."

Titanus threw many punches but couldn't find him. The klaxonbot sang its song, marking the end of the round.

There were very few places where Titanus wasn't oozing thick, Veritassian blood.

◆◆◆

Nervously, Prax and Blatt talked up Titanus's chances in the fight. Prax offered encouragement. "Little known fact: As a relative unknown, house odds had been stacked against him from the beginning. The odds of him winning the title were so astronomical that the Ministry of Applied Math and Formulas had to travel laterally to a neighboring multiverse to borrow additional numbers."

"What do you think they are now?"

"Between dismal and completely fucked. And not just for Titanus," said Prax as he telekinetically pointed a pen at the Emperor's platform. The monarch was demonstrating his apparent disappointment of the current performance of his champion by throwing random subjects to their death.

Back in his corner, Titanus was getting patched up. Lacerations and bruises covered his chest, torso, and skull. His thick red skin hid most of the blood, but the cameras could see it and so could the crowd. Methil buzzed around his ample frame, applying a styptic pencil to any wound he could find.

"Keep at it, Tits, you're wearing him down," he said.

"I am running out of time," Titanus said, adjusting his pinching codpiece.

"I know," said the coach. "But I believe in ya, kid. I bet all of my credits on you. You win, and I can finally open that scrapbooking shop—on my own planet populated only by Vuvlvanian geishas. Those bitches have four mouths and eight tongues."

"Let's think about now before later, Methil."

"Eight tongues! Imagine the possibilities!"

◆◆◆

Titanus delivered a lucky but devastating haymaker that sent Massst flying, knocking him into a wall. He staggered but was able to regain his composure before Tiffany could find a home in his chest.

Now tiring, both fighters moved strategically, neither overextending their reach. For all of his bravado, Massst knew that one more solid hit from the Veritassian meant death. He waited and made Titanus close the distance, hoping that the constant movement would sap what little energy his opponent had left.

The crowd became restless. The lack of immediate violence forced them to find it amongst themselves as arguments and trash talk gave way to vicious beatings, plasma weapons, and random lynchings. In response, the Emperor's guard released viral agents and triggered two small atomic weapons. Fortunately, with a billion in attendance, there were still enough fans alive to fill the lower platforms.

Their attention returned to the fight when Massst finally made a critical move.

By the end of the nineteenth round, Titanus had grown impatient and attempted another Reverse Pulverizer. There had been a method to the madness of Massst's avoidance hustle and flow. He had been studying Titanus closely and could now predict exactly how and where he would send his punches.

And more importantly, which way Tiffany would swing. In a sudden and unseen movement, Massst severed Titanus's sword hand, sending the charmed weapon to the ground.

"No!" screamed the sword. "Pick me up!"

"Fuck you, bitch!" responded Massst, kicking the sword into a far off storm drain. "See you never."

Tiffany's cries of protest faded away as she fell away into the dark unknown. Titanus stared at the nub that used to be his hand and wrist. Blood gushed with convulsive force and it took a combination of Methil firing a rocket launcher at the scoreboard and the dire need for a commercial break for the round to end.

Methil was able to cauterize the savage wound, but there would be little he could do for the loss of blood.

◆◆◆

Titanus leaned back on his stool. The world around him rippled, shimmering in and out. Methil threw out some encouraging words, but they had no effect, as all he heard was the ringing in his ears. He knew his body had very little left to offer. Whispering from deep within him, the spry Ragers swam with anticipation of his demise.

"I have reached my limit. I have failed."

Methil shook him vigorously. "Tits, I need you to focus." Methil grabbed a rusty bucket and produced a dripping sponge from it.

"No. Don't bother to wipe me down. I want the crowd and the Emperor to see my sacrifice."

Methil slapped him across the face. "I ain't giving you a sponge bath, dumbass. Hold out your hand." He gently placed the sponge in Titanus's outstretched palm. "Squeeze tight, big guy."

The sponge was not soaked in water. As the juice pushed out of the sponge, Titanus realized that it was a message from Hiediiee. As the fluid pressed through his fingers, he felt her love and longing.

Her pride for him.

Her sadness.

Her conviction.

Her understanding.

Her strength.

His heart raced, and with each beat, he understood the full complexity of her secretions as he experienced a deluge of memories, from the moment the met at the Petersbee Galactic aquarium, to her subsequent escape. He remembered fighting with his parents who condemned his love for a squid. There was the joy of birth, of little Tinyanus, and the handful of years he had been a loving father and husband.

In one bucket, all that they had ever been sloshed about, a soup made of their life together. Greedily he slammed the sponge into the bucket, coating himself with every drop he could absorb with the sponge. It was time to do what he came to do.

"For my wife and son," he said.

◆◆◆

The horn sounded. The fight was back on. Prax and Blatt immediately flew back to position. The crowd began to chant. The Emperor applauded with childlike vigor.

"PAX TITANUS!"

"PAX TITANUS!"

"PAX TITANUS!"

Titanus shooed Methil away and stood. He cracked his neck and stretched out his shoulders. Slamming his simple iron helm atop his head, he pointed to the crowd with his four muscular arms, nub and all.

"This will be the final round," he said.

The mighty warrior went into the twentieth round swinging and kicking. But for all of his fierce attacks he could not find his target. The clever Massst was always one step ahead of him. At one quarter the size of the mighty Titanus, he continued to use his quickness to predict the position of his enemy and simply swung his blade.

Slash! Slash! Slash!

Titanus had blindly walked into a brutal opening attack. Blood gushed from gashes from head to toe. Undaunted, he kept swinging. He was tempted to increase in size, but that would just give his foe more target area.

Slash! Kerrrang!

Although Titanus couldn't see it, Massst's blade clanged off of his helmet. Frustrated, the crowd screamed for him to at least land one blow. An opponent that didn't square off fairly in a fight such as Massst was universally despised, even if they all secretly had bet on the Kakuian to win.

Slash!

The shoulder.

Slash!

The thigh.

Slash!

The forearm.

Massst blinked in and out, to and fro, his blade flashing and carving more chunks out of his confused opponent. Titanus howled, his rage nearly causing the spontaneous ignition of his growth abilities.

Methil screamed from the far end of the arena. "Stop trying to hit him where he is! Hit him where he ain't!"

Titanus kept swinging. Massst kept stabbing. The crowd began to murmur in concern. It wouldn't be long now. The champion of the people was about to be undone by a Kakuian. They thought they were so great, those fucking one-second Kakuians, and now it was going to be true.

Titanus rolled onto his back. The hot, packed dirt of the arena floor comforted him even as Massst danced above, flitting in and out, sticking his steel here, there, and everywhere. His vision narrowed. It became hard to breathe.

There was only one option left.

Enlarge.

Enlarge!

ENLARGE!

Titanus concentrated all of his remaining energy to defiantly lift his one unwounded appendage, his cock. Clenching his fists, he commanded his cells to expand. With a rush, his mighty pole swelled in size, splitting his codpiece down the middle and firing toward the sky. Massst responded by snaking his way up the tower of flesh, keeping busy with his blade.

Deep within, the Ragers stirred. Electrified by the sudden burst of Titanus's power, they multiplied in response and raced through his system. Buried deep within his flesh and muscle, a conglomeration of malevolent lumps pushed their way out, causing massive boils and bumps to bubble and froth across his lacerated and bleeding hide. The adrenaline rush that came from the use of his powers gave way to a strange, narcotic calm. Titanus took his massive arm and feigned a tap out.

Sensing an impending victory, Massst ended his attack and stood on his opponent's chest, waiting to the referee to call the match. Exultant, he relaxed his time shift so that he could gloat and appear in focus for the millions of photos that would soon document his dominance in the arena.

He would not get the chance for glory.

The crowd gasped as they watched Titanus explode into a black cloud of swarming worms. Raining down upon the arena, the worms targeted Massst, latching onto him. The cocky Kakuian stared in horror as they began to burrow into his flesh.

He howled, the silent arena only making his futile screams all the more sickening.

Panicked, Massst blinked forward in time but that would not save him. Advancing the Ragers' growth cycle, it only made him die one second sooner. A second and larger puff of worms erupted where he once stood, coating the arena in a layer of Rager infection.

No one would forget Titanus or what happened after.

Prax and Blatt laughed about the expression on Massst's face for years. They were suckers for anything even remotely resembling physical comedy.

CHAPTER
TWENTY-TWO

Methil handed Hiediiee the helm that Titanus had worn in the fight. She unfurled her smallest tentacle and gently wrapped it around one of his spindly arms. She coated him with her appreciation.

"Ah, lady, it was my honor to coach your husband. I never told him, but I knew exactly what was at stake. How's the little one?"

She pulled him down the hall and they stopped outside Tinyanus's door. A small version of father, the boy played with action figure replicas of Titanus and the other gladiators.

"Just wait till my dad cracks your skull and grinds your bones to dust!" he chirped.

Methil eyes began to water. "Fucking great kid. Anyway, I wanted you to know that I made a shitload of money off of the fights. I always bet on Tits, even at the end."

Hiediiee secreted confusion.

Methil understood. "Yeah, one would think I would have lost it all when he died, but I placed another bet. The Kamari are crazy with the bookmaking and on a whim, I wagered that a Buster Bomb would destroy the planet. When the Ragers infected the crowd, they had no choice. Only four people escaped, those sportscasters, the Emperor, and me. And those dumbass rebels," Methil said as he pointed to Tinyanus's room, "the ones who kidnapped your boy? Their leadership was on-planet and were incinerated in the blast."

Methil rubbed his stomach with excitement. "The rest of them were executed the next day. The Emperor was pissed." Methil pointed at Tinyanus. "And with their summoning contract broken, the Dream Leeches moved on. They don't really care to kidnap children. I'm sure they hated it the whole time. Happy fucking ending."

Hiediiee hugged him goodbye, knowing he would be safely scrapbooking with his Vulvanian geishas soon. She floated back to Tinyanus's room and watched him play. It was over. Looking down at his bright, open eyes, and knowing that he was finally safe from the Dream Leeches, she gushed in relief.

Why, she simply oozed happiness.

Tom Lucas was born and raised in Detroit, and although currently enjoying the lack of snow and ice in Florida, remains a son of the post-industrial apocalypse.

He is a college professor and the author of the surreal novel *Leather to the Corinthians.*

Tom has been published in *Writer's Digest, The South End, The Oakland Press, The Macomb Daily, Orbit, Anthropomorphic,* and *U. Magazine.* He has also been featured the literary journals *The Write Place at the Write Time, Graffiti Rag, F*cked Up Fairy Tales,* and *Dark Fire Fiction.*

When not writing, Tom likes to drive fast and take chances.

For more information visit: http://readtomlucas.com/ and http://churchofthebigredj.com/

Bizarro Books

CATALOG   SPRING 2013

ERASERHEAD
PRESS

Your major resource for the bizarro fiction genre:

WWW.BIZARROCENTRAL.COM

Introduce yourselves to the bizarro fiction genre and all of its authors with the Bizarro Starter Kit series. Each volume features short novels and short stories by ten of the leading bizarro authors, designed to give you a perfect sampling of the genre for only $10.

BB-0X1
"The Bizarro Starter Kit"
(Orange)
Featuring D. Harlan Wilson, Carlton Mellick III, Jeremy Robert Johnson, Kevin L Donihe, Gina Ranalli, Andre Duza, Vincent W. Sakowski, Steve Beard, John Edward Lawson, and Bruce Taylor.
236 pages $10

BB-0X2
"The Bizarro Starter Kit"
(Blue)
Featuring Ray Fracalossy, Jeremy C. Shipp, Jordan Krall, Mykle Hansen, Andersen Prunty, Eckhard Gerdes, Bradley Sands, Steve Aylett, Christian TeBordo, and Tony Rauch. **244 pages $10**

BB-0X2
"The Bizarro Starter Kit"
(Purple)
Featuring Russell Edson, Athena Villaverde, David Agranoff, Matthew Revert, Andrew Goldfarb, Jeff Burk, Garrett Cook, Kris Saknussemm, Cody Goodfellow, and Cameron Pierce **264 pages $10**

BB-001 "The Kafka Effekt" D. Harlan Wilson — A collection of forty-four irreal short stories loosely written in the vein of Franz Kafka, with more than a pinch of William S. Burroughs sprinkled on top. **211 pages $14**

BB-002 "Satan Burger" Carlton Mellick III — The cult novel that put Carlton Mellick III on the map ... Six punks get jobs at a fast food restaurant owned by the devil in a city violently overpopulated by surreal alien cultures. **236 pages $14**

BB-003 "Some Things Are Better Left Unplugged" Vincent Sakwoski — Join The Man and his Nemesis, the obese tabby, for a nightmare roller coaster ride into this postmodern fantasy. **152 pages $10**

BB-005 "Razor Wire Pubic Hair" Carlton Mellick III — A genderless humandildo is purchased by a razor dominatrix and brought into her nightmarish world of bizarre sex and mutilation. **176 pages $11**

BB-007 "The Baby Jesus Butt Plug" Carlton Mellick III — Using clones of the Baby Jesus for anal sex will be the hip sex fetish of the future. **92 pages $10**

BB-010 "The Menstruating Mall" Carlton Mellick III — "The Breakfast Club meets Chopping Mall as directed by David Lynch." - Brian Keene **212 pages $12**

BB-011 "Angel Dust Apocalypse" Jeremy Robert Johnson — Meth-heads, man-made monsters, and murderous Neo-Nazis. "Seriously amazing short stories..." - Chuck Palahniuk, author of Fight Club **184 pages $11**

BB-015 "Foop!" Chris Genoa — Strange happenings are going on at Dactyl, Inc, the world's first and only time travel tourism company. "A surreal pie in the face!" - Christopher Moore **300 pages $14**

BB-032 **"Extinction Journals" Jeremy Robert Johnson** — An uncanny voyage across a newly nuclear America where one man must confront the problems associated with loneliness, insane dieties, radiation, love, and an ever-evolving cockroach suit with a mind of its own. **104 pages $10**

BB-037 **"The Haunted Vagina" Carlton Mellick III** — It's difficult to love a woman whose vagina is a gateway to the world of the dead. **132 pages $10**

BB-043 **"War Slut" Carlton Mellick III** — Part "1984," part "Waiting for Godot," and part action horror video game adaptation of John Carpenter's "The Thing." **116 pages $10**

BB-047 **"Sausagey Santa" Carlton Mellick III** — A bizarro Christmas tale featuring Santa as a piratey mutant with a body made of sausages. 124 pages $10

BB-048 **"Misadventures in a Thumbnail Universe" Vincent Sakowski** — Dive deep into the surreal and satirical realms of neo-classical Blender Fiction, filled with television shoes and flesh-filled skies. **120 pages $10**

BB-053 **"Ballad of a Slow Poisoner" Andrew Goldfarb** — Millford Mutterwurst sat down on a Tuesday to take his afternoon tea, and made the unpleasant discovery that his elbows were becoming flatter. **128 pages $10**

BB-055 **"Help! A Bear is Eating Me" Mykle Hansen** — The bizarro, heartwarming, magical tale of poor planning, hubris and severe blood loss... **150 pages $11**

BB-056 **"Piecemeal June" Jordan Krall** — A man falls in love with a living sex doll, but with love comes danger when her creator comes after her with crab-squid assassins. **90 pages $9**

BB-058 "The Overwhelming Urge" Andersen Prunty — A collection of bizarro tales by Andersen Prunty. **150 pages $11**

BB-059 "Adolf in Wonderland" Carlton Mellick III — A dreamlike adventure that takes a young descendant of Adolf Hitler's design and sends him down the rabbit hole into a world of imperfection and disorder. **180 pages $11**

BB-061 "Ultra Fuckers" Carlton Mellick III — Absurdist suburban horror about a couple who enter an upper middle class gated community but can't find their way out. **108 pages $9**

BB-062 "House of Houses" Kevin L. Donihe — An odd man wants to marry his house. Unfortunately, all of the houses in the world collapse at the same time in the Great House Holocaust. Now he must travel to House Heaven to find his departed fiancee. **172 pages $11**

BB-064 "Squid Pulp Blues" Jordan Krall — In these three bizarro-noir novellas, the reader is thrown into a world of murderers, drugs made from squid parts, deformed gun-toting veterans, and a mischievous apocalyptic donkey. **204 pages $12**

BB-065 "Jack and Mr. Grin" Andersen Prunty — "When Mr. Grin calls you can hear a smile in his voice. Not a warm and friendly smile, but the kind that seizes your spine in fear. You don't need to pay your phone bill to hear it. That smile is in every line of Prunty's prose." - Tom Bradley. **208 pages $12**

BB-066 "Cybernetrix" Carlton Mellick III — What would you do if your normal everyday world was slowly mutating into the video game world from Tron? **212 pages $12**

BB-072 "Zerostrata" Andersen Prunty — Hansel Nothing lives in a tree house, suffers from memory loss, has a very eccentric family, and falls in love with a woman who runs naked through the woods every night. **144 pages $11**

BB-073 **"The Egg Man" Carlton Mellick III** — It is a world where humans reproduce like insects. Children are the property of corporations, and having an enormous ten-foot brain implanted into your skull is a grotesque sexual fetish. Mellick's industrial urban dystopia is one of his darkest and grittiest to date. **184 pages $11**

BB-074 **"Shark Hunting in Paradise Garden" Cameron Pierce** — A group of strange humanoid religious fanatics travel back in time to the Garden of Eden to discover it is invested with hundreds of giant flying maneating sharks. **150 pages $10**

BB-075 **"Apeshit" Carlton Mellick III** - Friday the 13th meets Visitor Q. Six hipster teens go to a cabin in the woods inhabited by a deformed killer. An incredibly fucked-up parody of B-horror movies with a bizarro slant. **192 pages $12**

BB-076 **"Fuckers of Everything on the Crazy Shitting Planet of the Vomit At smosphere" Mykle Hansen** - Three bizarro satires. Monster Cocks, Journey to the Center of Agnes Cuddlebottom, and Crazy Shitting Planet. **228 pages $12**

BB-077 **"The Kissing Bug" Daniel Scott Buck** — In the tradition of Roald Dahl, Tim Burton, and Edward Gorey, comes this bizarro anti-war children's story about a bohemian conenose kissing bug who falls in love with a human woman. **116 pages $10**

BB-078 **"MachoPoni" Lotus Rose** — It's My Little Pony... *Bizarro* style! A long time ago Poniworld was split in two. On one side of the Jagged Line is the Pastel Kingdom, a magical land of music, parties, and positivity. On the other side of the Jagged Line is Dark Kingdom inhabited by an army of undead ponies. **148 pages $11**

BB-079 **"The Faggiest Vampire" Carlton Mellick III** — A Roald Dahl-esque children's story about two faggy vampires who partake in a mustache competition to find out which one is truly the faggiest. **104 pages $10**

BB-080 **"Sky Tongues" Gina Ranalli** — The autobiography of Sky Tongues, the biracial hermaphrodite actress with tongues for fingers. Follow her strange life story as she rises from freak to fame. **204 pages $12**

BB-081 **"Washer Mouth" Kevin L. Donihe** - A washing machine becomes human and pursues his dream of meeting his favorite soap opera star. **244 pages $11**

BB-082 **"Shatnerquake" Jeff Burk** - All of the characters ever played by William Shatner are suddenly sucked into our world. Their mission: hunt down and destroy the real William Shatner. **100 pages $10**

BB-083 **"The Cannibals of Candyland" Carlton Mellick III** - There exists a race of cannibals that are made of candy. They live in an underground world made out of candy. One man has dedicated his life to killing them all. **170 pages $11**

BB-084 **"Slub Glub in the Weird World of the Weeping Willows"** **Andrew Goldfarb** - The charming tale of a blue glob named Slub Glub who helps the weeping willows whose tears are flooding the earth. There are also hyenas, ghosts, and a voodoo priest **100 pages $10**

BB-085 **"Super Fetus" Adam Pepper** - Try to abort this fetus and he'll kick your ass! **104 pages $10**

BB-086 **"Fistful of Feet" Jordan Krall** - A bizarro tribute to spaghetti westerns, featuring Cthulhu-worshipping Indians, a woman with four feet, a crazed gunman who is obsessed with sucking on candy, Syphilis-ridden mutants, sexually transmitted tattoos, and a house devoted to the freakiest fetishes. **228 pages $12**

BB-087 **"Ass Goblins of Auschwitz" Cameron Pierce** - It's Monty Python meets Nazi exploitation in a surreal nightmare as can only be imagined by Bizarro author Cameron Pierce. **104 pages $10**

BB-088 **"Silent Weapons for Quiet Wars" Cody Goodfellow** - "This is high-end psychological surrealist horror meets bottom-feeding low-life crime in a techno-thrilling science fiction world full of Lovecraft and magic..." -John Skipp **212 pages $12**

BB-089 "Warrior Wolf Women of the Wasteland" Carlton Mellick III
— Road Warrior Werewolves versus McDonaldland Mutants...post-apocalyptic fiction has never been quite like this. **316 pages $13**

BB-091 "Super Giant Monster Time" Jeff Burk — A tribute to choose your own adventures and Godzilla movies. Will you escape the giant monsters that are rampaging the fuck out of your city and shit? Or will you join the mob of alien-controlled punk rockers causing chaos in the streets? What happens next depends on you. **188 pages $12**

BB-092 "Perfect Union" Cody Goodfellow — "Cronenberg's THE FLY on a grand scale: human/insect gene-spliced body horror, where the human hive politics are as shocking as the gore." -John Skipp. **272 pages $13**

BB-093 "Sunset with a Beard" Carlton Mellick III — 14 stories of surreal science fiction. **200 pages $12**

BB-094 "My Fake War" Andersen Prunty — The absurd tale of an unlikely soldier forced to fight a war that, quite possibly, does not exist. It's Rambo meets Waiting for Godot in this subversive satire of American values and the scope of the human imagination. **128 pages $11**

BB-095 "Lost in Cat Brain Land" Cameron Pierce — Sad stories from a surreal world. A fascist mustache, the ghost of Franz Kafka, a desert inside a dead cat. Primordial entities mourn the death of their child. The desperate serve tea to mysterious creatures. A hopeless romantic falls in love with a pterodactyl. And much more. **152 pages $11**

BB-096 "The Kobold Wizard's Dildo of Enlightenment +2" Carlton Mellick III — A Dungeons and Dragons parody about a group of people who learn they are only made up characters in an AD&D campaign and must find a way to resist their nerdy teenaged players and retarded dungeon master in order to survive. **232 pages $12**

BB-098 "A Hundred Horrible Sorrows of Ogner Stump" Andrew Goldfarb — Goldfarb's acclaimed comic series. A magical and weird journey into the horrors of everyday life. **164 pages $11**

BB-099 "Pickled Apocalypse of Pancake Island" Cameron Pierce—A
demented fairy tale about a pickle, a pancake, and the apocalypse. **102 pages $8**

BB-100 "Slag Attack" Andersen Prunty— Slag Attack features four visceral,
noir stories about the living, crawling apocalypse.A slag is what survivors are calling the slug-like maggots raining from the sky, burrowing inside people, and hollowing out their flesh and their sanity. **148 pages $11**

BB-101 "Slaughterhouse High" Robert Devereaux—A place where
schools are built with secret passageways, rebellious teens get zippers installed in their mouths and genitals, and once a year, on that special night, one couple is slaughtered and the bits of their bodies are kept as souvenirs. **304 pages $13**

BB-102 "The Emerald Burrito of Oz" John Skipp & Marc Levinthal
—OZ IS REAL! Magic is real! The gate is really in Kansas! And America is finally allowing Earth tourists to visit this weird-ass, mysterious land. But when Gene of Los Angeles heads off for summer vacation in the Emerald City, little does he know that a war is brewing...a war that could destroy both worlds. **280 pages $13**

BB-103 "The Vegan Revolution... with Zombies" David Agranoff —
When there's no more meat in hell, the vegans will walk the earth. **160 pages $11**

BB-104 "The Flappy Parts" Kevin L Donihe—Poems about bunnies, LSD,
and police abuse. You know, things that matter. **132 pages $11**

BB-105 "Sorry I Ruined Your Orgy" Bradley Sands—Bizarro humorist
Bradley Sands returns with one of the strangest, most hilarious collections of the year. **130 pages $11**

BB-106 "Mr. Magic Realism" Bruce Taylor—Like Golden Age science fic-
tion comics written by Freud, *Mr. Magic Realism* is a strange, insightful adventure that spans the furthest reaches of the galaxy, exploring the hidden caverns in the hearts and minds of men, women, aliens, and biomechanical cats. **152 pages $11**

BB-107 **"Zombies and Shit" Carlton Mellick III**—"Battle Royale" meets "Return of the Living Dead." Mellick's bizarro tribute to the zombie genre. **308 pages $13**

BB-108 **"The Cannibal's Guide to Ethical Living" Mykle Hansen**— Over a five star French meal of fine wine, organic vegetables and human flesh, a lunatic delivers a witty, chilling, disturbingly sane argument in favor of eating the rich.. **184 pages $11**

BB-109 **"Starfish Girl" Athena Villaverde**—In a post-apocalyptic underwater dome society, a girl with a starfish growing from her head and an assassin with sea anenome hair are on the run from a gang of mutant fish men. **160 pages $11**

BB-110 **"Lick Your Neighbor" Chris Genoa**—Mutant ninjas, a talking whale, kung fu masters, maniacal pilgrims, and an alcoholic clown populate Chris Genoa's surreal, darkly comical and unnerving reimagining of the first Thanksgiving. **303 pages $13**

BB-111 **"Night of the Assholes" Kevin L. Donihe**—A plague of assholes is infecting the countryside. Normal everyday people are transforming into jerks, snobs, dicks, and douchebags. And they all have only one purpose: to make your life a living hell.. **192 pages $11**

BB-112 **"Jimmy Plush, Teddy Bear Detective" Garrett Cook**—Hard-boiled cases of a private detective trapped within a teddy bear body. **180 pages $11**

BB-113 **"The Deadheart Shelters" Forrest Armstrong**—The hip hop lovechild of William Burroughs and Dali... **144 pages $11**

BB-114 **"Eyeballs Growing All Over Me... Again" Tony Raugh**— Absurd, surreal, playful, dream-like, whimsical, and a lot of fun to read. **144 pages $11**

BB-115 **"Whargoul" Dave Brockie** — From the killing grounds of Stalingrad to the death camps of the holocaust. From torture chambers in Iraq to race riots in the United States, the Whargoul was there, killing and raping. **244 pages $12**

BB-116 **"By the Time We Leave Here, We'll Be Friends" J. David Osborne** — A David Lynchian nightmare set in a Russian gulag, where its prisoners, guards, traitors, soldiers, lovers, and demons fight for survival and their own rapidly deteriorating humanity. **168 pages $11**

BB-117 **"Christmas on Crack" edited by Carlton Mellick III** — Perverted Christmas Tales for the whole family! . . . as long as every member of your family is over the age of 18. **168 pages $11**

BB-118 **"Crab Town" Carlton Mellick III** — Radiation fetishists, balloon people, mutant crabs, sail-bike road warriors, and a love affair between a woman and an H-Bomb. This is one mean asshole of a city. Welcome to Crab Town. **100 pages $8**

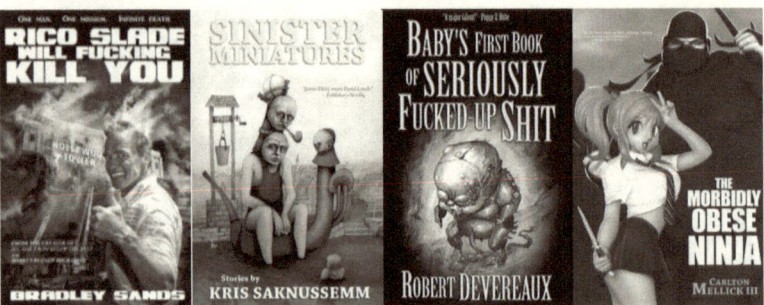

BB-119 **"Rico Slade Will Fucking Kill You" Bradley Sands** — Rico Slade is an action hero. Rico Slade can rip out a throat with his bare hands. Rico Slade's favorite food is the honey-roasted peanut. Rico Slade will fucking kill everyone. A novel. **122 pages $8**

BB-120 **"Sinister Miniatures" Kris Saknussemm** — The definitive collection of short fiction by Kris Saknussemm, confirming that he is one of the best, most daring writers of the weird to emerge in the twenty-first century. **180 pages $11**

BB-121 **"Baby's First Book of Seriously Fucked up Shit" Robert Devereaux** — Ten stories of the strange, the gross, and the just plain fucked up from one of the most original voices in horror. **176 pages $11**

BB-122 **"The Morbidly Obese Ninja" Carlton Mellick III** — These days, if you want to run a successful company . . . you're going to need a lot of ninjas. **92 pages $8**

BB-123 **"Abortion Arcade" Cameron Pierce** — An intoxicating blend of body horror and midnight movie madness, reminiscent of early David Lynch and the splatterpunks at their most sublime. **172 pages $11**

BB-124 **"Black Hole Blues" Patrick Wensink** — A hilarious double helix of country music and physics. **196 pages $11**

BB-125 **"Barbarian Beast Bitches of the Badlands" Carlton Mellick III** — Three prequels and sequels to *Warrior Wolf Women of the Wasteland*. **284 pages $13**

BB-126 **"The Traveling Dildo Salesman" Kevin L. Donihe** — A nightmare comedy about destiny, faith, and sex toys. Also featuring Donihe's most lurid and infamous short stories: *Milky Agitation, Two-Way Santa, The Helen Mower, Living Room Zombies,* and *Revenge of the Living Masturbation Rag.* **108 pages $8**

BB-127 **"Metamorphosis Blues" Bruce Taylor** — Enter a land of love beasts, intergalactic cowboys, and rock 'n roll. A land where Sears Catalogs are doorways to insanity and men keep mysterious black boxes. Welcome to the monstrous mind of Mr. Magic Realism. **136 pages $11**

BB-128 **"The Driver's Guide to Hitting Pedestrians" Andersen Prunty** — A pocket guide to the twenty-three most painful things in life, written by the most well-adjusted man in the universe. **108 pages $8**

BB-129 **"Island of the Super People" Kevin Shamel** — Four students and their anthropology professor journey to a remote island to study its indigenous population. But this is no ordinary native culture. They're super heroes and villains with flesh costumes and out-landish abilities like self-detonation, musical eyelashes, and microwave hands. **194 pages $11**

BB-130 **"Fantastic Orgy" Carlton Mellick III** — Shark Sex, mutant cats, and strange sexually transmitted diseases. Featuring the stories: *Candy-coated, Ear Cat, Fantastic Orgy, City Hobgoblins,* and *Porno in August.* **136 pages $9**

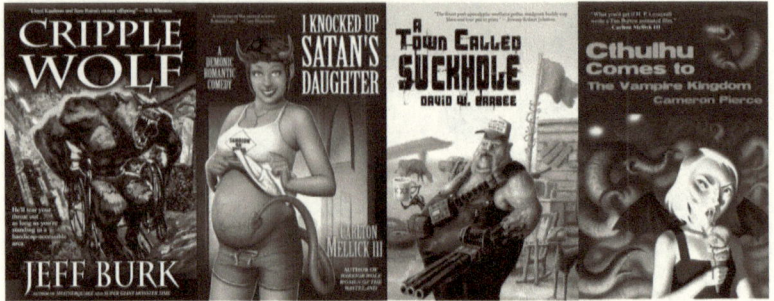

BB-131 **"Cripple Wolf" Jeff Burk** — Part man. Part wolf. 100% crippled. Also including *Punk Rock Nursing Home, Adrift with Space Badgers, Cook for Your Life, Just Another Day in the Park, Frosty and the Full Monty*, and *House of Cats*. **152 pages $10**

BB-132 **"I Knocked Up Satan's Daughter" Carlton Mellick III** — An adorable, violent, fantastical love story. A romantic comedy for the bizarro fiction reader. **152 pages $10**

BB-133 **"A Town Called Suckhole" David W. Barbee** — Far into the future, in the nuclear bowels of post-apocalyptic Dixie, there is a town. A town of derelict mobile homes, ancient junk, and mutant wildlife. A town of slack jawed rednecks who bask in the splendors of moonshine and mud boggin'. A town dedicated to the bloody and demented legacy of the Old South. A town called Suckhole. **144 pages $10**

BB-134 **"Cthulhu Comes to the Vampire Kingdom" Cameron Pierce** — What you'd get if H. P. Lovecraft wrote a Tim Burton animated film. **148 pages $11**

BB-135 **"I am Genghis Cum" Violet LeVoit** — From the savage Arctic tundra to post-partum mutations to your missing daughter's unmarked grave, join visionary madwoman Violet LeVoit in this non-stop eight-story onslaught of full-tilt Bizarro punk lit thrills. **124 pages $9**

BB-136 **"Haunt" Laura Lee Bahr** — A tripping-balls Los Angeles noir, where a mysterious dame drags you through a time-warping Bizarro hall of mirrors. **316 pages $13**

BB-137 **"Amazing Stories of the Flying Spaghetti Monster" edited by Cameron Pierce** — Like an all-spaghetti evening of Adult Swim, the Flying Spaghetti Monster will show you the many realms of His Noodly Appendage. Learn of those who worship him and the lives he touches in distant, mysterious ways. **228 pages $12**

BB-138 **"Wave of Mutilation" Douglas Lain** — A dream-pop exploration of modern architecture and the American identity, *Wave of Mutilation* is a Zen finger trap for the 21st century. **100 pages $8**

BB-139 **"Hooray for Death!" Mykle Hansen** — Famous Author Mykle Hansen draws unconventional humor from deaths tiny and large, and invites you to laugh while you can. **128 pages $10**

BB-140 **"Hypno-hog's Moonshine Monster Jamboree" Andrew Goldfarb** — Hicks, Hogs, Horror! Goldfarb is back with another strange illustrated tale of backwoods weirdness. **120 pages $9**

BB-141 **"Broken Piano For President" Patrick Wensink** — A comic masterpiece about the fast food industry, booze, and the necessity to choose happiness over work and security. **372 pages $15**

BB-142 **"Please Do Not Shoot Me in the Face" Bradley Sands** — A novel in three parts, *Please Do Not Shoot Me in the Face: A Novel*, is the story of one boy detective, the worst ninja in the world, and the great American fast food wars. It is a novel of loss, destruction, and--incredibly--genuine hope. **224 pages $12**

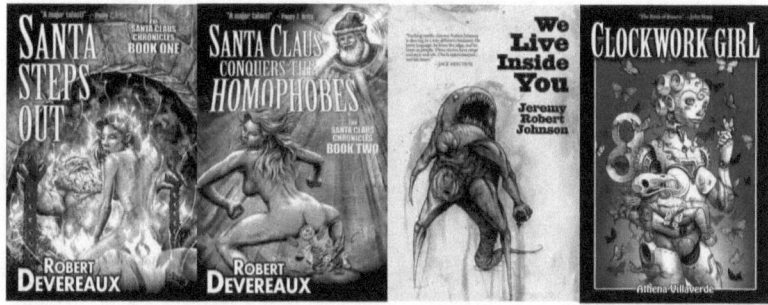

BB-143 **"Santa Steps Out" Robert Devereaux** — Sex, Death, and Santa Claus ... The ultimate erotic Christmas story is back. **294 pages $13**

BB-144 **"Santa Conquers the Homophobes" Robert Devereaux** — "I wish I could hope to ever attain one-thousandth the perversity of Robert Devereaux's toenail clippings." - Poppy Z. Brite **316 pages $13**

BB-145 **"We Live Inside You" Jeremy Robert Johnson** — "Jeremy Robert Johnson is dancing to a way different drummer. He loves language, he loves the edge, and he loves us people. These stories have range and style and wit. This is entertainment... and literature."- Jack Ketchum **188 pages $11**

BB-146 **"Clockwork Girl" Athena Villaverde** — Urban fairy tales for the weird girl in all of us. Like a combination of Francesca Lia Block, Charles de Lint, Kathe Koja, Tim Burton, and Hayao Miyazaki, her stories are cute, kinky, edgy, magical, provocative, and strange, full of poetic imagery and vicious sexuality. **160 pages $10**

BB-147 **"Armadillo Fists" Carlton Mellick III** — A weird-as-hell gangster story set in a world where people drive giant mechanical dinosaurs instead of cars. **168 pages $11**

BB-148 **"Gargoyle Girls of Spider Island" Cameron Pierce** — Four college seniors venture out into open waters for the tropical party weekend of a lifetime. Instead of a teenage sex fantasy, they find themselves in a nightmare of pirates, sharks, and sex-crazed monsters. **100 pages $8**

BB-149 **"The Handsome Squirm" by Carlton Mellick III** — Like Franz Kafka's *The Trial* meets an erotic body horror version of *The Blob*. **158 pages $11**

BB-150 **"Tentacle Death Trip" Jordan Krall** — It's *Death Race 2000* meets H. P. Lovecraft in bizarro author Jordan Krall's best and most suspenseful work to date. **224 pages $12**

BB-151 **"The Obese" Nick Antosca** — Like Alfred Hitchcock's *The Birds*... but with obese people. **108 pages $10**

BB-152 **"All-Monster Action!" Cody Goodfellow** — The world gave him a blank check and a demand: Create giant monsters to fight our wars. But Dr. Otaku was not satisfied with mere chaos and mass destruction.... **216 pages $12**

BB-153 **"Ugly Heaven" Carlton Mellick III** — Heaven is no longer a paradise. It was once a blissful utopia full of wonders far beyond human comprehension. But the afterlife is now in ruins. It has become an ugly, lonely wasteland populated by strange monstrous beasts, masturbating angels, and sad man-like beings wallowing in the remains of the once-great Kingdom of God. **106 pages $8**

BB-154 **"Space Walrus" Kevin L. Donihe** — Walter is supposed to go where no walrus has ever gone before, but all this astronaut walrus really wants is to take it easy on the intense training, escape the chimpanzee bullies, and win the love of his human trainer Dr. Stephanie. **160 pages $11**

BB-155 **"Unicorn Battle Squad" Kirsten Alene** — Mutant unicorns. A palace with a thousand human legs. The most powerful army on the planet. **192 pages $11**

BB-156 **"Kill Ball" Carlton Mellick III** — In a city where all humans live inside of plastic bubbles, exotic dancers are being murdered in the rubbery streets by a mysterious stalker known only as Kill Ball. **134 pages $10**

BB-157 **"Die You Doughnut Bastards" Cameron Pierce** — The bacon storm is rolling in. We hear the grease and sugar beat against the roof and windows. The doughnut people are attacking. We press close together, forgetting for a moment that we hate each other. **196 pages $11**

BB-158 **"Tumor Fruit" Carlton Mellick III** — Eight desperate castaways find themselves stranded on a mysterious deserted island. They are surrounded by poisonous blue plants and an ocean made of acid. Ravenous creatures lurk in the toxic jungle. The ghostly sound of crying babies can be heard on the wind. **310 pages $13**

BB-159 **"Thunderpussy" David W. Barbee** — When it comes to high-tech global espionage, only one man has the balls to save humanity from the world's most powerful bastards. He's Declan Magpie Bruce, Agent 00X. **136 pages $11**

BB-160 **"Papier Mâché Jesus" Kevin L. Donihe** — Donihe's surreal wit and beautiful mind-bending imagination is on full display with stories such as All Children Go to Hell, Happiness is a Warm Gun, and Swimming in Endless Night. **154 pages $11**

BB-161 **"Cuddly Holocaust" Carlton Mellick III** — The war between humans and toys has come to an end. The toys won. **172 pages $11**

BB-162 **"Hammer Wives" Carlton Mellick III** — Fish-eyed mutants, oceans of insects, and flesh-eating women with hammers for heads. Hammer Wives collects six of his most popular novelettes and short stories. **152 pages $10**